DARK SIBLING

Carrie J Keaton

Dark Sibling
Copyright © 2022 by Carrie J Keaton

ISBN
978-1-957895-18-5 (Paperback)
978-1-957895-19-2 (eBook)

Contents

Chapter

One

"*I hate you Lina… you b-i-t-c-h! Everybody seems to like you so damn much. I don't know what everyone sees in you that's so fucking great. It's always, she so sweet… she's so nice… she's so smart. Well you know what big sister? I can't stand your ass. I hate you Lina! I hate you!*" Those were the hurtful, spiteful words Danielle screamed at Melina the last time she'd seen her right after their father's funeral before Danielle drove away.

Melina shuddered at the thought of the final words her little sister had said to her as she sat by her bay window staring out at the park across the way. She couldn't believe that it had been close to sixteen years since her kid sister Danielle had been vacant from her life and had not shown any affection toward her.

Melina stood up from her kitchen table and walked over to the end table near the couch and retrieved her family album. A stray tear coursed down her saddened face as she remembered some of the not so happy memories while growing up with her little sister back in the day. After seating herself on the couch, she slowly began thumbing through the pages of her family album, reminiscing back on something she had read quite some time earlier in a magazine. The words that resonated through her mind were *"Sisters hold each other's hands for a little while. But they hold each other's hearts forever."*

Melina believed that one should be truly thankful to have each other as sisters and enjoy each other's company as much as possible. But as far as her younger sister Danielle, this woman that she calls her sister and who is her sister by blood has turned into someone who is not there for her at all, this woman she calls sister is someone who doesn't care for her at all, this woman that she call sister, intentionally tries to hurt her, makes her cry, and is never there for her when times are blue, this woman that she calls sister, isn't true to her or herself, this woman that she calls sister, by choice she longs to be able to call her a best of friend, this woman that she calls sister, will never be there for her till the end, this woman that she calls sister, she has prayed for her to be a blessing from God above, but this woman that she calls sister, she believes will always remain in her heart as the little sister that she'll always love.

Melina's daughter Nikki bounding in the front door interrupted the insightful thoughts and brought her back to reality. Nikki was now a sixteen year-old who had turned into quite a compassionate and articulate young lady.

"Mama, I'm home," she yelled.

Melina quickly wiped her face because she didn't want her daughter to see her crying. She and Nikki were so close that she would probably still notice that something was bothering her mother even though she tried to hide it well. Her daughter knew her so well and they have a very close and loving relationship.

"What are you doing Mama," she asking plopping down on the couch beside her.

"Just looking through this family album and thinking of my sister Danielle," Melina says displaying her most convincing, best smile.

"Mama, didn't you tell me that Aunt Dannie and you had a kind of bad misunderstanding?" Nikki asked innocently.

"Yes, we did have a rather bad fallout many years ago baby girl. We had one our most heated altercations when I was probably about your age and it was about a boy I was dating in high school."

"Really Mama? Did Aunt Dannie try to steal your boyfriend?"

She paused for a moment and observed her beautiful daughter's angelic face. She was as intelligent as she was beautiful. She was also quick to understand the essence of whatever her mother would tell her and of things that she didn't tell her and was able to "fill in the blanks" to complete whatever words she was about to say or was thinking. There weren't many who could pull one over on her. Melina could talk to her openly about things because of her intellect. She understood about '*the birds and the bees*' concept before I had spoken to her about it.

"Yes, your Aunt Dannie did try to take my boyfriend and she succeeded too. Of course my boyfriend was as much to blame as she was. I don't know why some guys are such dogs and cheats. They tend to be motivated by sex — new sex, more sex, different sex and will sleep with anyone — even my own sister. But my sister intentionally wanted to hurt me. She went out of her way to make sure that I found out that she had slept with my boyfriend. I felt so betrayed by Danielle. I won't forget what she did to me but I did eventually forgive her. You know, when you are wounded by betrayal, it does stick with you. However, I didn't want my sister's betrayal to come between us. So I forgave her so that we could try to move forward."

"I understand what you are saying Mama. You were trying to hold on to your relationship with Aunt Dannie and also she is your only sister. I don't think I have seen my aunt but a couple times in my whole life so I really don't know her very well."

"I know sweetheart and I'm so sorry that you never had an opportunity to establish a relationship with your aunt," I said remorsefully. "I really do wish that things could have been different."

"Mama, maybe one day Aunt Dannie will come around and want to be a part of our lives. But until then, you got me," Nikki said throwing her arms around my neck.

"I'm going upstairs to do homework so I will see you later Mama," Nikki said, kissing me on the cheek and then turning to go upstairs.

Melina was so proud of Nikki. She had turned into such a responsible, loving, and compassionate young woman. Their relationship was not perfect but it was a great one. She played parent first and friend second. The two of them definitely did not see eye to eye on everything; she is a teenager after all! But Melina always thanked God that Nikki was much better than most teens. And, as her daughter pointed out to her quite often, her mom was not known for an automatic "yes" every time she asked her for something. But, at the end of the day, they loved each other and that's what counts.

Remembering back when she'd had *"the talk"* with Nikki, Melina smiled contently. Talking about menstruation with her daughter wasn't as bad as she thought it might be and she ended up starting her period at age thirteen. But Melina wanted to find a way to mark the beginning of menstruation for her and to recognize and celebrate this rite of passage in her daughter's life. Almost every woman remembers how she got her first period. She thought that this would be a good opportunity to create a positive memory for her daughter, as this was an important milestone meaning that her daughter had started growing into a woman. Melina decided on three things that she thought would make this occasion special for her; she took Nikki shopping, treated her to lunch and she had written her a letter. She had gotten the idea of writing the letter from reading this article in Lifestyle magazine. It was written by Paul Sloane and Vanessa Leigh. The article made so much sense that she wanted to share it with her teen-age daughter. For Melina, the article needed to have special meaning for their occasion. So it ended up being a "Letter of Motherly Advice" kind of thing. The letter went like this:

A Letter to my Daughter: Motherly Advice

Dear Nikki,

> *I wanted to take this moment right now to tell you about something on my mind and in my heart. So I am telling you about something very important to me.*

I don't think it is possible that I could love you any more than I do. You are so dear and special to me, and dear and special don't even begin to cover what is in my soul. The thought of you brings tears to my eyes; just because of how meant to be it was for you to come to us. The angels definitely delivered you to our door that is for sure! You are a true gift from heaven. And, I absolutely adore being a mom -- being your mom. I loved being your mommy, for sure, but being a mom is pretty swell also.

When your age hit double digits, it was a very difficult transition for me. It reminded me how much you were growing up. Too fast for me, no matter how slow at times the years have gone. I have grown accustomed to you wanting to do things yourself, without help, and am trying to not call you any babyish nicknames in public, nor show any displays of affection in front of your friends. But, this year starts the challenge for me with the tug between holding on and letting go.

Hold on, because you are still my child, my baby, my little girl that I brought into the world. You are fragile, and vulnerable, and the world can be a dangerous place. Hold on, because life is difficult, your heart will get broken, you will have disappointments and fears and tragedy. I need to keep you close.

Let go, because you are becoming a young woman. You are a fantastic student, musician, dancer, writer, artist, and humanitarian. You have made both of us so proud in your short thirteen years of life so far, and there are so many more triumphs to go. You are capable, and confident, and determined to have whatever it is in this world that you desire. I know that no matter what obstacles may get in your way, you will always forge your own path and walk, and sometimes run, toward your destiny, whether that is five minutes or five days from home. I trust that you will know how to make those hard decisions as you grow older, and that you will be wise and balanced.

Today, I consider how difficult that balance is, between holding on and letting go. I read a friend's book that she wrote years ago, called Peaceful Parenting. Her name is Nancy Buck, and it is based on the concept of Choice Theory psychology, as to why humans behave the way that they do.

What I take from her book the most and has benefitted me as a parent is her premise that throughout a child growing up, they and their parents continuously pass through alternating cycles of competitiveness and cooperation. Getting along and conflicting with each other --Mutuality and dissention. That describes our days and months as you grow older to a tee.

And, I know that we can all handle it. For at the base of all of this conflict and all of this cooperation and all of this holding on and letting go, is the deepest love I have ever encountered. That love that we have for one another, the three of us, is simply the fabric that will keep us all together. Through the triumph, tragedy, good, bad, joy and sorrow. It will help us to know when to let go, and when to hold on.

I love you so much, my beloved daughter. I know that your life will be as sweet for you as you have made it for us. Remember always, my little angel girl, how truly blessed we are to have you.

You are a wonderful person and your father and I think the world of you. It will not be long before you leave home to make

*your way in the world. Can I please give
you some friendly, motherly advice? Here
are some things that you should never do.*

1. Never Despise Yourself.

You are great and capable of achieving great things so believe in yourself. When things go badly, never stop believing. Some girls get depressed, blame themselves and lose self-esteem. All sorts of problems can follow.

2. Never Get Obsessed with your Appearance.

We think you look great (though some of the outfits you wear worry us!). Please be happy with the person you are and the body you have. Eat sensibly, exercise and be healthy. Some girls become obsessed with losing weight or getting the perfect shape. You are and look beautiful to us.

3. Never Live Beyond Your Means.

Throughout life, try to keep spending within your income and so save a little. Avoid getting into debt if possible. There are some exceptions - like getting a mortgage to buy a house - but generally if you can live within your means you will avoid all sorts of problems.

4. Never Compromise Your Personal Safety.

Never put yourself at serious risk. This means that you cannot trust people until you really know them and that sometimes you have to avoid things that look like they might be fun. Never get drunk or take drugs. Unfortunately there are some malevolent people out there and it is best not to take undue risks.

5. Never Get Involved with a Married Man.

There are plenty of great single men out there. Don't get entangled with a married man no matter how attractive he is - it will end in your tears.

6. Never Give Less Than Your Best.

We are very proud of what you have accomplished so far. You should be proud too. Keep doing well. Keep trying your hardest at everything you do. No one can ask for more than that.

7. Never Forget that Your Parents Love You.

Whatever happens in life, your family will still be your family. Whatever difficulties you encounter you can always talk to us and we will try to help. We are here for you if the need ever arises, you can always come home.

Loving you Always,
Mom

Melina had felt anxious and indecisive about educating her daughter about sex. When she finally did have the "birds and the bees" talk, it went exceptionally well with her daughter. Though schools often include sex education in the curriculum — they might also impart some information about Aids and pregnancy. She believed that as a parent, too, she should be involved with educating her child about these issues of physical health, and about the moral aspects of sexual behavior. She wanted to prepare Nikki for puberty so that she would not be caught with her proverbial pants down. Melina offered her information in small doses rather than in one "big talk.

Melina also believed that a mother/daughter relationship was very important. It is one of the most important relationships in life. All she wanted was for her daughter to live happy and excel in life. She had all these expectations for her daughter, that she would be great in whatever she undertook and would make her proud. This is very much true in many mother daughter relationships. For Melina to reach a stage that she can be proud of, she needed to ensure that she brought up her daughter in a manner that she would be proud of. Their relationship began when she conceived. She knew instinctively that she was carrying a girl. When Melina realized that she was in fact carrying a girl, she wanted to be in a position to prepare mentally and emotionally for her arrival.

Melina believed that most women felt blessed when they were anticipating having a girl. This was the time that you started to build on a relationship because she used to talk to Nikki before she was born. She felt this went a very long way in helping her create this bond that the two of them share now and it would last a lifetime.

Melina felt all mothers should know that understanding is the key word. She learned to be patient with her child. All that she had invested in her since she was little played a pivotal role as to how she has turned out today. She helped to strengthen their relationship when she was young. Otherwise, it would be pretty hard to instill wisdom when she is all grown up.

She tried to teach her daughter how to treat others with respect and understand the value of wisdom and hard work. Melina believed that there was nothing more fulfilling like knowing your special bond between you and your daughter could not be broken.

Melina had for so long wished that she had a close-knit relationship with her sister Dannie as she did with her daughter Nikki. She and her daughter could talk about anything. Her relationship with her daughter and her husband Grant were the two people who she loved with all her heart and they're the ones who have helped to fill much of the void left by her sister's absence. She had met and married Grant Harrington right out of college. After a few years, the two of them had been blessed with Nikki. But Melina still tries to remain optimistic that one day Dannie will want to be in her life again.

Chapter

Two

Melina and her husband Grant for the most part have had a wonderful relationship and had met each and fell in love while they both were in college in Nebraska. Melina had attended The University of Nebraska-Lincoln where she had gotten her masters in occupational therapy. Grant had attended University of Nebraska at Omaha where he earned a master in electrical engineering degree. The two of them married a few years after both had graduated and decided to make their home in Lincoln, Nebraska.

They have had ups and downs as any other couple has but they have always been able to communicate with each other and work things out. They had made a promise to each other on their wedding night that they would never go to bed angry at each other. So far, they have managed to keep that promise.

Lincoln, the State Capitol of Nebraska, has an approximate population of 220,000. It is the home of the University of Nebraska-Lincoln, Nebraska Wesleyan University, Union College, Southeast Community College and several private vocational-technical schools. The business of the city centers on government, education, insurance/banking and light industry.

Melina's husband Grant works as an electrical engineer here in Lincoln, Nebraska. He specializes in power distribution for both commercial and industrial facilities, works with the design of power & lighting systems and performs engineering calculations, equipment sizing, selection and layout, and leads design efforts on these projects. He is highly sought after as he has a great work record in contractual assignments. Sometimes he's sent out of town on assignments and could be away for weeks at a time, but the jobs always paid great.

Melina specializes in physical and occupational therapy and speech therapy and work at Homestead Health & Rehabilitation Center. It has been a very rewarding job and she's a qualified professional who is trained and dedicated to providing care for those with these special needs. This center is actually a beautiful place. With gorgeous grounds, it's private with enclosed courtyards and fountains; the facility is located on eight acres in a residential neighborhood, they offer private rehabilitation suites, there are three separate dining rooms with restaurant style dining, and it has a on-site beauty salon. The state of the art therapy equipment and home-like environment helps to make its residents feel more "at home". Her job didn't require her to have to leave town but she did work a lot ---- sometimes seven days a week when needed.

As rewarding as her job was, she still wished that she had a relationship with Danielle. She remembered that life had not always been easy for them when they were growing up, but things could have been so much better and easier if through it all they had their love for each other to bring them comfort.

Melina and Grant had managed to build a strong relationship and it was held together by their love for each other. The product of that love was Nikki, their beautiful daughter who was the light of their lives. There were disagreements between the two of them sometimes but they weathered the storms together very graciously. They managed to create a sense of safety that allows each of them to feel comfortable expressing his/her feelings, problems, and dissatisfactions. This sense of safety has been a part of the foundation upon which they negotiated things that bothered them. Each of them came into this relationship with certain expectations about how things were to be. But without the ability to communicate and negotiate, any issues that should rise would turn into a power struggle that almost always damaged the relationship.

Some couples just seem to have that extra something that made their marriage great and Melina didn't know exactly what their secrets to being happily married couples were but she and Grant had built trust over the years. They were apart quite often due to his job, but the two of them had always made the most of their time together. For more than fifteen years they had gone to bed together. In their eyes, going to bed at the same time showed that they wanted to experience the closeness that can only be found in bed. Melina had found that some of their best conversations occurred with her head on her husband's shoulder lying in bed. Her husband liked to stay up later than she did, but he also liked to cuddle with her in bed. So sometimes he would go to bed with her and then get back up after they'd had their cuddle time.

Melina and her husband have shared interests such as supporting the Big Brothers Big Sisters Organization. Big Brothers Big Sisters is the nation's premiere donor and volunteer-supported youth mentoring organization and they both loved helping kids who were less fortunate. Sharing our interests and ideas with their life partner was one of the things they did during their quality time together. Before they had Nikki, she and her husband enjoyed four-wheeling in his jeep.

Melina and Grant still hold hands because they feel that holding hands shows that they are still in love and that they cherish just touching their partner and need that connection whether they are walking through a store or just sitting on the couch.

Sometimes she and Grant had a hard time trying to stay focused on the positive. Melina believed that remaining positive was very important to their marriage. You know we all have something that we dislike about our spouses whether it is that he bites his fingernails or maybe it's that she spends too much money on clothes. When you are happy you focus more on the positive things about your spouse than the negative and you look not at the few things your spouse do wrong instead you'll see all of the things that they do right.

One of the hardest things to do was to learn to forgive. But Melina and Grant learned to forgive freely and forgive each other. Not only did they forgive each other, but they also did not bring up past mistakes and throw them in each other's faces. Once the misdeed was forgiven it was also forgotten.

The simple three little words, "I love you," was a very important sentence for Melina and Grant as they try to tell each other daily. When they say the words they are reminding each other and reaffirming the love that they feel. Both of them communicated with each other in order to stay connected. Communication was a necessity. If you can't talk to each other, you won't stay together very long. They shared the good things and tried to discuss problems without getting angry. Melina and Grant also tried to talk to each other throughout the day. They communicated through email and phone calls during the day and then always took time to talk to each other every evening.

Sometimes Melina's and her husband would disagree, and that's when compromising came into play. If both of them kept trying to learn to give, then both would be happy for the most part. They gave affection to each other through hugs, kisses, and touching, and they felt that it was important because it created a bond and kept the romantic feelings alive. They both tried to respect the other's needs and their desires. Their mutual respect for each other meant that consideration was taken for the others feelings.

Their daughter Nikki was a junior in Lincoln High School. She was a high achiever, had made the honor roll consistently, and had been nominated by many of her teachers for Student of the Month. Students of the Month were nominated by their teachers on the basis of their consistent good effort, their determination and perseverance, their passion for learning, their integrity and, when applicable, notable improvement in their work. A Recognition Committee was established a long time ago to advocate for and facilitate greater recognition of student academic and service excellence. This committee consists of one or two parents of students from each academic year, two IHS teachers, one IHS administrator and ideally, an Immaculate Parents Association liaison member.

Departments each month are invited to nominate students from each grade level, if possible, for recognition as their Student of the Month. Each staff member in the department may submit up to four nominations: one for each grade. When forms are submitted, the students are assigned a code number that becomes the sole identifier of the nominee for the Recognition Committee until it has reached a consensus. All discussions and decisions are made solely on the basis of the teacher's description of the specific merits of a nominee.

Lincoln High teaches all students a rigorous academic core. The students are urged to follow as challenging an academic program as possible in order to develop their God-given talents to the fullest, to increase their opportunities for admission to the college of their choice, and to enhance their options and potential for success in college and in life.

This high school itself was founded in 1871 and is the oldest of the six public high schools in the city of Lincoln, Nebraska. It is also one of the oldest high schools in Nebraska. The present building was opened in 1915 with major additions completed in 1927, 1957, 1985 and 1996. In over 130 years of service to the community, more than 40,000 students have graduated from LHS. The school colors are red and black and the mascot is the "Links".

Lincoln High school serves approximately 1,750 students in grades 9-12. 650 students live outside the Lincoln High attendance area and have chosen to attend Lincoln High. It has 150 certified staff members (over half have advanced degrees) and 90 support staff members who help with the operation of the building each day. Lincoln High is accredited by the North Central Association and has the AA accreditation rating of the Nebraska State Board of Education. In 1984 it was named a "Recognized School of Excellence" by the U.S. Department of Education.

Lincoln High School students have experienced success in almost every area. In the past ten years 40 National Merit Semifinalists have been named. Many LHS athletic teams regularly qualify for state tournaments with the Boys Basketball team winning several championships. The band has received superior ratings in all recent competitions. Students have regularly placed well in state and national competitions in vocational programs, speech, debate, and student council. The One-Act Play won the State Championship.

Melina was impressed with the Mission Statement of Lincoln High, *"Lincoln High School is committed to preparing each student to use multiple perspectives and individual talents to live, learn, and work in a diverse society. "*

She respected the school and what it represented and her daughter Nikki for doing such a wonderful job in school. She was so very proud of her daughter because this was what she had tried so hard to instill in her – to love, live, laugh, and work hard in life.

Chapter

Three

Lincoln is also the county seat of Lancaster County and the home of the University of Nebraska. Lincoln, located on the Great Plains far from the moderating influence of mountains or large bodies of water, possesses a highly variable four-season humid continental climate: winters are cold but relatively dry; summers are hot and occasionally humid. With little precipitation falling during winter, precipitation was concentrated in the warmer months, when thunderstorms frequently roll in, often producing tornadoes. Snow tended to fall in light amounts, though blizzards were possible. Snow cover was not very reliable due to both the dryness and the frequent thaws during winter.

It was a fine Saturday morning — so fine that you would scarcely have believed that the few months of Lincoln's summer had yet flown by. The City of Lincoln is the capital and the second-most populous city of the US state of Nebraska.

Hedges, fields, and trees presented to the eye their ever-varying shades of deep rich green; scarce a leaf had fallen; scarce a sprinkle of yellow mingled with the hues of summer warned you that autumn had begun. The sky was cloudless, the sun shone out bright and warm; the songs of birds, and hum of myriads of summer insects, filled the air; and the park gardens, crowded with flowers of every rich and beautiful tint, sparkled, in the heavy dew, like beds of glittering jewels. Everything bore the stamp of summer, and none of its beautiful colors had yet faded from the dye.

Melina and Grant were to work on one of their volunteer projects today. Volunteerism wasn't just for older children or single people to spend their time being productive. It also gave couples an opportunity to strengthen their partnership by giving back to their communities. Couples working side-by-side volunteering their services created a special bonding between them. They can support and encourage each other while reaping the personal accomplishments together. The satisfaction of helping others is better shared with someone you love.

The Harringtons were working with HandsOn Lincoln (HOL) was a non-profit organization connecting volunteers with service opportunities, facilitating volunteer work for 737 Middle Nebraska nonprofits, schools, government agencies, faith-based organizations, civic groups and businesses. HOL volunteers support 25 issue areas ranging from hunger and homelessness to at-risk youth and seniors in need.

By the end of the day both Melina and Grant were ready for a change of scenery. The two of them went home and decided to treat themselves to a night out and dinner at a nice restaurant to celebrate their hard work.

Nikki and Xandria were preparing to leave when Melina and Grant got home. Their daughter kissed them both at the door and told them that she and Xandria were going to take in a movie and that she would see them tomorrow. Nikki had never given them and ounce of trouble and has always been very responsible plus they loved Xandria as if she was their daughter too. Grant and Melina told them to be careful, to not be out too late, and that they loved them both.

Grant and Melina showered and dressed for their outing. When Grant's eyes fell upon Melina, he knew he was in deep trouble the moment she opened the bedroom door. His gaze took in the outfit she'd chosen to wear. It was a black, clingy number that flaunted everything it concealed. The way the dress fit her body reminded him of just how enticing all of her body parts were, covered or uncovered. The dress ended way above her knees with slits on both sides showing long, gorgeous legs. He swallowed deeply. There was no doubt that tonight would be one he'd remember for a long time.

"Ready to go, Grant. I just need to grab my purse," Melina said mischievously and reminding him that he was there for some reason other than to stand in the doorway and ogle her.

"Yeah, sure," he said, watching as she disappeared into the back. He wiped a bead of sweat from his brow with his hand. Things were heating up already. He glanced up when she reentered the room.

"I'm ready," she said, placing the strap of her purse on her shoulder. "And you never did say where we were going."

He gazed into her dark eyes and responded. "I thought it would be nice if we drove to the Venue Restaurant and Lounge. I heard that they're a nice seafood restaurant and I know how much you like seafood."

Melina's smile widened. She was glad he'd decided to take her there because she did adore seafood – especially snow crab.

"Sounds great, but first I think we should get this out of the way," she said taking a step closer and wrapping her arms around his neck. "You know – we start all of our days out this way so we may as well stay on a roll, don't you think?" she whispered silkily before joining her mouth to his.

Closing her eyes, she settled her body against his, immediately feeling him get hard against her. When he opened his mouth beneath hers she slipped her tongue inside and decided to play "catch me if you can."

He caught her, tangling her tongue with his and feasting on her mouth like a starving man. The more he feasted, the more her body began overflowing in desire so thick she could almost smother in it. When he reached down and touched her hips to bring her more snugly against him, slanting his mouth across hers in the process, she decided to pull back before they ended up making love on their living room floor. The woman knew just what buttons to punch and how to punch them.

Melina was getting herself hot and bothered too. Fighting the heat erupting in her stomach, Melina licked her lips as if relishing in the taste of him but she knew that she needed to bring things to an abrupt halt if they planned on going to dinner tonight. Tilting her head up, she smiled brightly. "All right then, I'm ready to go."

Incapable of speech, Grant could only nod and follow her out the door.

When Melina and Grant arrived at the Venue Restaurant and Lounge, it was easy to see why it was such a wonderful, highly-recommended place for dining.

The restaurant provided the ultimate experience for every patron that visited their establishment through premium service, quality, and atmosphere. The Venue combined three exciting entities into one location.

Whether you are dining in, carrying out, enjoying libations in the lounge, or utilizing their conference/party room, patrons could count on getting the best venue has to offer every time they walked through their doors.

When their meal was delivered, Melina turned eating snow crabs into the most erotic sight Grant ever saw. She had taken her tongue and practically sucked and licked the claws dry. The motions she had made with her mouth while eating the crabs had him shifting in his seat. He could just imagine the things that she could do with that mouth, which was something he was now anticipating to come later.

"Do you think you're going to want dessert?" Melina asks sexily.

Her question grabbed his attention and their gazes met and held across the table. Yes, he wanted dessert, but what he had a sweet tooth for was definitely not on the menu.

He took several deep breaths before answering. "No, I think I'll pass, but you can order something if you'd like."

She smiled. "Thanks. I see on the menu that they have ice cream cones. I think I'll order one since I feel like licking something tonight."

His erection suddenly strained against his zipper with such brutal force that he nearly gasped in pain. "Then by all means order one," he said huskily, surprised that he was capable of speech.

Her smile widened. "I think I will."

Grant thought that in all his thirty-five years he had never seen anyone lick an ice cream cone like she did. Sitting across from her and watching her tongue at work was enough to tempt him to have more than one glass of wine, but since he was the one doing the driving he just sat there and let her torture him. Besides, he had a feeling he needed all his faculties to handle the rest of the evening with Melina, and couldn't help wondering how she intended it to end.

After he'd taken care of their check, he stood. "Ready to leave?"

"Yes."

He nodded. He would find out soon enough.

When she stood, intense longing flared through him as he took a look at her dress, and seeing what he could of her dark creamy flesh was enough to make him lose control. "Have I told you how good you look tonight?"

Even her chuckle turned him on. "Yes, four times tonight. Thanks. And you know what they say, don't you?"

He raised a curious dark brow. "No, what do they say?"

"They say that flattery will get you everywhere."

He tilted his lips in a smile when he thought of all the possibilities. "Everywhere?"

"Grant -- I have an idea. Let's do something spontaneous. Let's go to Midland Beach."

"Uh – uh – uh okay, whatever you want Melina," Grant stuttered.

As so as Melina had gotten into the vehicle she begun twitching in her seat saying her back needed scratching. A wicked smile adorned Grant's face as he slowly unzipped Melina dress. He was more than happy to oblige until his fingers had come into contact with her bare skin. The first thing he'd noted was the absence of a bra. The next thing had been how warm and smooth her skin was.

His hand had glided over the spot she'd indicated needed scratching. The throaty sounds she'd made when he'd finally found the spot had sent shivers of excitement racing down his spine. If she made those kinds of sounds from having her body scratched, he didn't want to imagine what type of sounds she would make when they made love.

"Are you sure your back feels better?" he asked once he had zipped her dress completely up.

She turned around in her seat. "Yes, I'm sure." She smiled and gave him a thoughtful look. "I'd almost forgotten what great hands you have."

"A-h-h," Melina moaned throatily. "Move just a little lower. Ahh, now move just a little more to the right; do it harder. Yes, oh yes, that's it, harder still. Umm, that feels so much better."

After one last moan she looked over her shoulder and said. "Thanks for scratching my back, Grant. You can zip me back up now."

Grant's hand trembled as he slowly zipped up Melina's dress.

Blood raced through his body at an alarming speed with the memories that suddenly came to mind. "I'm glad I was able to help you to remember," he said as his fingers absently stroked the steering wheel. "We shared some wonderful times together back then, didn't we?"

Once they arrive at Midland beach, Melina got out of the vehicle, removed her pumps and tosses them back in, and strode down by the shoreline.

"Come on Grant," she calls back to him.

Grant removes his shoes, socks, rolls up each of his trouser legs, grabs a huge beach towel and quickly catches up to her.

The night air was cool and Melina began to shiver slightly as she walked along the shoreline. Grant removes his shirt and drapes it over her shoulders for warmth. The moon's glow seemed endless and bathed the beach waters in a sparkling hue.

She stopped for a moment and drew in a calming breath and inhaled the scent of the water. A number of stars sparkled overhead like dots of diamonds in a dark velvety sky. Grant had walked on ahead of her several feet and had stopped to watch a skimmer that was flying low over the water. The reflection from the moon provided enough light for her to see Grant very well who was standing less than twenty feet away, staring out at the ocean.

She gathered the shirt against her chest and just stood there transfixed and watched him, knowing he was unaware of her staring at him. The shimmering light cast his features into sharp view, and she thought that she had never seen a more beautiful specimen of a man. The only piece of clothing he wore was his black trousers and the rich brown coloring of his skin seemed to glow. His bare chest, masculine shoulders, and firm thighs displayed a physically fit body, one that was capable of giving a woman intense pleasure. She shuddered, remembering just what kind of pleasure it could deliver.

Heated desire thrummed through her already hot veins as her body responded to the sheer essence of him, making it plainly clear whom it wanted and what it needed.

She inhaled deeply and the sound seemed to alert Grant to her admiration of him. He turned, and his gaze caught hers and held it. Heat flowed from his eyes to her and the desire in his eyes communicated to her, making every nerve in her body move between her legs. She shuddered against the sexual power he held over her from just looking at her.

His gaze said it all. He wanted her.

Melina took a step forward, knowing that she wanted him, too. She bit her lip, remembering how things have always been between them, the heat and the intensity.

She watched Grant take the remaining steps toward her, holding her gaze all the while. The expression on his face was intense, and for a moment she could only imagine what thoughts were flitting through his mind. Then suddenly, she read a few of them and her breath caught and her nipples hardened. He planned on doing a lot to her tonight; and no matter how he tried, he still wouldn't get enough.

Without saying a single word, he leaned down and kissed each corner of her mouth before hungrily staking his claim and slanting his mouth over hers. He could feel her breathing quicken and the heat that flooded her mouth when he felt her body shudder. He felt it vibrate through every cell, every pulse, every pore.

Grant's tongue was in control, and Melina's went where his led, seeking, devouring, eating away at her with a hunger that made her knees weaken and her heart race. She wrapped her arms around him, feeling the hardness of him, large and physical. His fingers slipped beneath the straps of her dress and pulled it down off her shoulders, and his mouth began devouring her breasts.

He was renewing his brand, staking a claim, reaffirming what had always been. His mouth moved back to hers, demanding her response as it greedily robbed her of any conscious thought other than how he was making her feel. And she matched him, passion for passion.

His hand moved to her hips and grasped her bikini bottom, and after one firm tug on the flimsy material it ripped. She broke the kiss, panting profusely. Her decision made, she took a step back and eased what was left of the bikini bottom down her legs and kicked it aside. She then pulled the dress over her head and tossed it away.

Naked, she went back into Grant's arms. "I want you," she whispered softly.

His mouth captured hers and he picked her up into his arms and walked her to the area where he had spread the beach towel only moments earlier. He placed her down on it, and then proceeded to remove his trousers.

Grant heard her breath catch when he stood before her, gloriously naked and aroused. He loved her and has always loved her. Loving her was what had made him whole.

His entire body was tensed, wired, filled with desire. And when she reached out her arms to him, he dropped down beside her on the towel, aroused and ravenous beyond reason.

Passion grew to extreme proportions when Grant's fingers touched Melina, skimming all over her body. The curves, fullness, and lushness he found absolutely extraordinary as he stroked her everywhere, beginning with her breasts before moving lower between her legs.

There his hand found the treasure he sought. She was hot to his fingers, exceedingly wet, and the scent of her consumed him. He began stroking her while whispering just what he wanted to do to her.

When neither of them could take any more, he knelt before her, driven to taste her all over. He began spreading kisses all over her body, paying special homage to her breasts, flicking his tongue over the swollen nipples. And when he heard her soft, throaty breath catch, he was determined to go lower.

Holding her hips firmly in his hand he lowered his mouth past her navel and felt her body clench in surprise, then heard the sounds of shocked pleasure that erupted from deep in her throat when his tongue delved into the very essence of her, loving it, cherishing it.

"Grant!"

His name was a scream of gratification when his tongue began stroking her in a way it had done many other times before. Taking his hand he gently widened her legs, determined to get everything he wanted. With the heat of his mouth he showed her just what she meant to him — what she'd always meant to him.

She screamed his name over and over as her nails clawed his back, and when he felt her body tense with her climax, he swiftly moved in place over her.

Their gazes met the moment his body entered hers as his hand grabbed her hips and lifted her to go deeper.

"A-h-h." He released a long sigh and a deep shuddering breath when her inner muscles tightened around him, clenching his throbbing erection, holding it captive inside of her. For a second he couldn't move; he just remained still in that position, savoring the feel of being inside of her, connected to her, one with her.

"Love me, Grant."

Her words broke him, destroyed the very last vestige of his control and restraint, opening a floodgate of desire. He began moving and the strokes increased. His mind began spinning out of control. His body followed, and when he felt her body let go as an orgasm shook her to the core, he screamed her name and pushed deeper inside of her as an orgasm tore through him as well, making him explode inside of her. Lowering his head, he consumed her lips, her mouth, and her tongue.

Too weak to move, Melina lay in Grant's arms, enjoying the feel of being there. When he shifted his body to stare down at her, she felt the intensity in his gaze. He leaned forward and captured her lips and she gloried in what they had shared.

He ran a finger along her eyelids and saw the tears lodged there. Reaching out she pulled him into her arms. "Let's go home, Grant," she whispered softly. She intended to show him just how much she loved him.

After taking a shower together to wash the beach sand from their bodies, Grant and Melina got into bed and made love again. This time she showed him just what he meant to her.

Grant leaned over in bed and tenderly cupped Melina's cheek in his hand. I could never stop loving you because you are such a part of me, a part I know that I will have with me no matter what.

A smile touched the corners of Melina's lips. "And what about when I get old and gray, Grant?" she asked teasingly, although the look in his eyes was serious.

"You will still be my love. I asked you to be my wife, my best friend, and my lover. We will be together forever." He pulled her closer into his arms. "I love you Melina – it's always you."

A sense of overwhelming happiness brought tears to Melina's eyes. "I love you Grant, too, and always will."

She reached up and caught the back of his head in her hand and pulled his mouth down to meet hers.

He groaned when their mouths made contact, and his arms automatically closed around her. Heat poured through every part of him as he gladly took what she offered.

Moments later, he drew back and broke off the kiss, dragging in a deep breath. He felt his erection get heavy and the need to be inside of her. "Look at me," he whispered huskily. "I want you to see just how you make me feel when I'm making love to you."

She gazed up at him when he placed his body over hers. His features revealed the intensity of how he felt when he was inside of her. She wrapped her arms around his neck and smiled.

"There's nothing like a lover's touch," she said breathlessly, when he began moving inside of her, setting a rhythm and igniting their passion once again.

And as he made love to her, he knew that her love and her touch were all he would ever need.

Chapter

Four

Grant arose early this Sunday morning and had left Melina asleep. He brewed some coffee, poured himself a cup, and went into the study. Reclining in his chair, his mind visited a time in his past that had been a turning point in his life. His mind suddenly went back to the first day he had ever laid eyes on Melina. He had been twenty, a junior in college and she had been seventeen and had just started college. That summer he had come to live with Ms. Minnie, an old family friend, the first year after his parents' death in an auto accident. After getting a part-time job as a lifeguard, he had gone to the optometrist's office in town to undergo the required eye exam. Melina had been working there as an assistant to the doctor, and from the first moment he saw her, he had been drawn to her like a moth to a flame.

Sighing deeply, he tried to compose himself when he finally came to a stop directly in front of her. "Melina!" He greeted her in a low husky voice that he almost didn't recognize as his own.

"Grant!" she said breathlessly, whether from the run or from startled surprise he wasn't sure. She met his intense gaze with one of her own. "You said you'd never come back. Why are you here?"

Her question made his thoughts shift to that ill-fated day three years ago when he had left town. At the time she was a seventeen-year old and felt that maybe she was confused. Maybe it had been just an infatuation and that she may have thought she had love feelings for Grant. Now she was a gorgeous woman at almost twenty and was everything male fantasies were made of.

His gaze did a slow burn down the length of her body. Her skimpy top and shorts made him very much aware of her bare thighs, long legs, curvy hips, and generous cleavage. His eyes then moved upward and zeroed in on her nut-brown face, which was more beautiful than ever. He knew her lips tasted just as good as they looked, full, ripe, and with a flavor that was distinctively hers.

Heat pooled low in his belly and his blood grew hot and heavy in his veins when he remembered the number of times his tongue had stroked those lips.

"Grant?"

He realized he hadn't answered her question and a part of him suddenly became obsessed with having the beautiful young woman he'd walked away from three years ago back in his life.

Feeling he had nothing to lose and everything to gain, he decided to show her rather than tell her why he had returned.

Melina didn't know what had happened. One moment she was staring at Grant, and the next moment she was wrapped firmly in his arms with his mouth devouring hers.

Her body stiffened, then relaxed as any thought of resisting him was destroyed the second his tongue entered her mouth, capturing hers and evoking memories she'd tried to suppress a few years earlier.

His mouth was hot and sweet to the taste. Even the light musky scent of his sweat was intoxicating. Waves of desire uncoiled inside of her as he stroked her tongue, making every emotion she had skate around in her brain. He'd always had this sort of effect on her, even when she'd been too young to understand what sexual chemistry was about.

The sudden feel of his tongue on hers made all-consuming heat ignite between her legs and she heard herself moaning deep in the back of her throat. He wrapped his fingers in her hair to hold her mouth in place, as if she could possibly think of going anywhere. Although logic ruled that indulging in this kind of kiss with him was crazy, she intended to get her fill now and criticize her act of foolishness later.

When the distant sound of the horn from a shrimp boat invaded, he slowly lifted his mouth from hers. It was then that she saw that at some point she had grabbed hold of his shoulders to keep from falling when her knees had weakened.

She slowly lowered her arms to her side and felt him untangle his fingers from her hair. She realized that any attempt to pretend she hadn't been affected by his kiss would be futile because she *had* been affected and had a feeling he knew it. The one thing they had never been able to hide from each other was desire. When it came to arousing her, he had the process down pat.

"Melina," he murmured, in a low, sexy drawl, recapturing her attention.

She drew in a steady breath as heat poured through her. He was well over six feet tall, had a nice build, and was the color of semisweet chocolate. At twenty-three he had aged handsomely and was still the kind of man who women, both young and old, noticed at first glance.

A deep frown came to her face when she remembered how easily he had walked away two years ago and not looked back, and the pain she had suffered. "Why, Grant? Why did you come back after all this time?"

He reached out and stroked his thumb across her bottom lip, a lip still tingling from their kiss. She hoped he didn't detect the hot, fiery desire that was running rampant inside of her; however, judging by the dark, hot look in his eyes, he did.

"I'd hope after that kiss the reason I'm back would be obvious, Melina," he said huskily in a deep voice that shook her to the core. "I came back for you."

Grant had been harboring an immoral secret from back in the day only Melina had no clue as to just how dark of a secret it was. The mere thought of how dishonorable it was zapped Grant's mind back to reality.

Chapter

Five

Melina's younger sister Danielle lived in Atlanta, Georgia. She had acquired a very nice one bedroom house in Virginia Highlands and it really was a great place. It was a large Craftsman Style home that had one bedroom with the bath upstairs and a great fireplace. The house was located just minutes to shopping areas such as Kroger, Publix Little Five Points, and Virginia Highlands. There were even several nice parks within walking distance in the neighborhood. The neighborhood also boasted prominent colleges close-by too such as Georgia Tech, Emory, SCAD or Georgia State.

Danielle was a client financial management professional for Accenture. She was a very intelligent woman with strong financial management, analytic and strategic skills, and also was strong in accounting and accounting principles. She was a first-class program and project manager, who understood teamwork and communicated well with people at all levels.

Danielle worked with many prestigious clients to provide them services from the opportunity phase through contract completion in the areas of GAAP compliance, internal controls, budgeting/forecasting, contract profit and loss management, and advisory services to customer leadership teams and corporate leadership.

She assisted with the preparation of engagement, project, and program reporting as well as Accenture internal financial accounting processes, executing or assisting with tracking and reporting of third-party out-of-pocket expenses, hardware/software costs, and client time and expenses against program budget, and any other expense charges to program budget monitoring or advising on engagement financial status and engagement capital assets and technology rental equipment, performing or assisting with reconciliation processes, data and report archiving, forecast management activities, and contract compliance.

Danielle had thrived from the power of her career and was sought out by many big businesses because she was great at her job. She had attained her bachelor's degree in accounting with an overall GPA of 4.0 and held a master's degree in Finance. After her internship with the Accenture, she excelled until she earned her promotion to financial officer with impeccable skills in financial accounting, reconciliation, invoice preparation, processing financial transactions, and preparing financial budgets, etc. She had done so well in that position that she was made head financial officer with the added responsibility of overseeing subordinate analysts within the company.

Danielle had carved out a wonderful life for herself financially and had a rewarding career. With all of her accomplishments in her life, she still loathed her older sister. The hatred she held for her sister had only grown and manifested over the years and it seemed that all she wanted was a chance to hurt Melina. This conflict was not the natural state of her and Melina's relationship, but this discord between the two of them had been sown early and had endured for most of their lives. Even though their parents had done their best at loving and respecting both of their children, Danielle seemed to continue drifting farther and farther away and distancing herself from the family.

Most siblings fought as kids, but Danielle had grown up and saw her sister as her worst enemy. She just refused to let go of the jealousy and bitterness that had been brewing within her since their childhood. She had committed some horrible acts against Melina over the years and has never attempted to apologize or accept any responsibility for anything she's ever done.

Danielle was now plotting to take the rivalry between her and Melina to a whole new level. She wanted to destroy her sister's happiness and her life and had devised a plan that she believed would do just that – destroy Melina's life. But Danielle had to get close to her sister in order to pull off this feat. After careful consideration of what she wanted accomplished, Danielle decided that she would have to fake a reconciliation between she and Melina. She knew that pretending to want a fresh start with her sister would be a hard thing to pull off – especially since she despised her. But this was a necessary step to get her where she needed to be in order to execute her plan.

It had been many years since Melina and Danielle had shared any pleasantries with each other, but Dannie was ready to put her plan into action right now. How would she pull off such a feat?

First she needed a credible explanation to be away from her job. After careful thought she tells the director of the company that she works at a very convincing lie in order to get excused extended leave. Danielle explains to the director that her older sister had been in a very bad car accident and that it was necessary for her to be there for her until she gets back on her feet. Danielle had already gotten a male friend who works at a hospital in Nebraska to forge a note from a doctor stating that it was medically necessary for her to be with her sister until she recovered. After presenting this note from a doctor to her boss, she was granted FMLA. The Family & Medical Leave Act (FMLA) allows employees to take off up to 12 work weeks in any 12 month period for the birth or adoption of a child, to care for a family member, or if the employee themselves has serious health condition. Danielle also put in for her vacation time which would give her an additional 12 weeks of time for a total of 6 months leave.

With all of her I's dotted and T's crossed, Danielle was ready to launch her plan to hurt her sister Melina. Her first plan of action was to place a phone call to her sister and tell her she wanted a fresh start. Danielle had officially declared war on Melina and let the chips fall where they may.

Chapter

Six

When Melina awoke this Saturday morning, she knew it would be one of those melancholy days that she would reminisce about her younger sister Danielle. Probably other sisters would have written her off by now, but she just couldn't do that to her. Maybe it has to do with the way that she's hard-wired because she just believed that there was hope that her little sister will want to make up with her and be a part of her life. God knows that she has missed her and longed to have a real sisterly relationship with her over the years. It is just so hard to believe that her own sister could hate her to the point that she didn't care how much it hurt her with the things that she did to her. Her sister Danielle didn't seem to care about how her spiteful, cruel words ripped up her sister's heart.

After getting up and dressing, Melina put on a pot of coffee, poured a glass of orange juice, and fixed a couple of bagels with strawberry cream cheese spread. Before seating herself at the kitchen table, she went and retrieved her photo album from the den. As she leisurely turned the album pages, her mind was flooded with memories of her childhood past with her sister Danielle. Between these pages were more than just treasured photos of her family, *this family album* had captured most of her family's heritage. As painful as some of the memories were, Melina could recall a few of the joyous times when her family members enjoyed each other and did things together. She had always heard that a picture could be worth 1000 words. In this album, some of the pictures were like evil ghosts of the past that stood as a reminder of much of the pain she had endured at the hands of a sister who cared for no one but herself.

Melina had finished eating her bagel and drank the remainder of her orange juice. So she got up and fixed a cup of coffee in which she added hazelnut creamer. She loved the flavor of hazelnut creamer in her coffee because it seemed to heighten the coffee drinking experience for her and it also tasted smooth and delicious.

"That coffee smells great Mama," her daughter Nikki said as she entered the kitchen.

"It tastes great too baby, do you want some?"

"Maybe just a half a cup Mama."

Nikki fixed her some coffee, grabbed a saucer and placed a bagel on it and spread a generous amount of the strawberry spread on it. She then pulled her chair around the table next to her mother and joined her looking through the photo album.

"Look Nikki, isn't this a cute picture of you when you were five?"

"Mama, come on. You would say that I was cute anyway just because you're my mama."

"You're right baby, I would say that, but it is the truth. You are such a beautiful young lady both inside and out."

"Okay Mama, enough of that mushy stuff. So -- why are you really looking through the album?" Nikki said showing a serious expression on her face.

"I was just thinking of your Aunt Dannie again and started going through this photo album."

"Didn't you say that Aunt Dannie was very mean to you when you all were growing up?"

"Yes, she had been down-right cruel to me and she had no reason to be."

"I don't understand how a sister could be that way Mama. I know that if I had a sister, she would definitely not be treated that way."

"I know that you wouldn't treat your sister badly sweetheart because you have such an enormous heart and it is filled with so much compassion. Your aunt Dannie crushed me with hurtful names all my life. There were a couple of times that she physically hurt me just because she could. She seemed to get kicks out it. However, the difference here is that my sister is beautiful on the outside and stunning, but on the inside, she was very ugly, evil-minded and selfish. There were many times that she had been asked to join modeling agencies but she never would commit. A big part in why she found it okay to bully me was because she had never been told the word "*NO*" and she should had been. She has gotten away with things that average people couldn't just because she was stunning and academically very bright. Sometimes on an odd occasion I asked her why she taunted me so, and she would answer. . I just wanted to make you miserable because I can't stand you."

"Nikki, all of the cruel things that your aunt said to me hurt badly but I still wanted to try to reach her. I loved my sister and just didn't want to give up on her just because she hurt me. So then I told Dannie I wanted her to do something about herself because I had heard stories that when you push someone in a certain way they change. I had an innate strength within myself, but on the outside I guess I still showed vulnerability and Dannie probably could see it. But I still tried to put on the front of being so strong so that she would know that if she hurt me, I could withstand it. I told her that all I wanted was to try to comfort her because she was so angry. I wanted to let her know that she was better than this awful sister that she was displaying before me – that she had been placed in my life as a force that will ultimately help me prevail and for her to just remember that. She just blasted me again with a lot of harsh, hurtful words and stormed off."

"Where does aunt Dannie live now Mama?" Nikki asked, creasing her brow with concern.

"Well – last I heard, Danielle moved to Atlanta, Georgia which was only about twenty miles from Marietta where we both grew up. They called Atlanta "the Hostess City" of the South. The city is vastly hip and culturally sophisticated and that was what appealed to your aunt. But Atlanta did manage to retain its southern charm as it's a large city of over 4.9 million people."

"Mama, I am so sorry aunt Dannie made you feel so badly. I realize now how strongly you feel about your sister, and I'm sorry that she torments you so. I just wish that I knew something that could give you some peace", Nikki said with tears in her beautiful brown eyes.

She threw her arms around her daughter and hugged her tight. Relief washed over her and it felt as though much of the pain and loneliness dissipated with that embrace.

"You have been such a wonderful blessing to me Nikki and I love you so much."

"I know Mama and I love you too", Nikki said after stepping back and kissing her mother's forehead. "Mama, I'm going to the mall for a little while and I should be back in a few hours. Do you need something?"

"No baby, I'm good", she replied smiling proudly. "You enjoy yourself".

"I'll have my cell phone with me so call if you think of something", Nikki said as she walked out the front door.

After Nikki had gone, Melina continued thumbing through the pages of her family album. She treasured some of the sweet old memories of her past a as time had gone swiftly by. A few of the memories brought smiles of happiness yet some tears to her eyes.

Melina and Danielle had grown up in Marietta, Georgia and it was such a beautiful place. Cobb County liked to market the area's recreational attractions by referring to itself as "the fun side of Atlanta," and Mariettans had spent hundreds of thousands of dollars sowing seeds and planting trees and shrubs to promote beautification throughout the city. The town square, bleached-white gazebos, and the antebellum mansions had given Marietta the misty feeling of the Old South. It was that "old South" charm and close proximity to Atlanta that made Marietta a great place to grow up. Our daddy worked at the Lockheed-Martin manufacturing plant and our mother did private in home care for the elderly. Our parents had given us a pretty great life and had tried to give us practically whatever we wanted even though Danielle seemed to never be pleased or happy about anything.

It has been said that the nicest people in the United States reside in Georgia. If you live there or have driven through the state, you know this is true. In fact, if you were from such areas as NYC, South Florida or California, Georgians are so polite compared to you that it can be somewhat disconcerting. Located in the foothills of the picturesque Blue Ridge Mountains, Marietta has numerous historical homes, monuments and sites. Just north of Atlanta, it has a population of about 68,000. The CSX freight trains between Atlanta and Chattanooga (Western & Atlantic Subdivision) still ran a block west of the town square, past the train depot (now the Visitor Center) and the Kennesaw House, one of only four buildings in Marietta not burned to the ground in Sherman's March to the Sea. The Kennesaw House was home to the Marietta Museum of History which tells the history of Marietta and Cobb County. Dobbins Air Reserve Base on the south side of town and a Lockheed-Martin manufacturing plant were among the major industries in the city.

Melina thought that it was kind of funny how some things seem to never leave the corner of your heart even when you try hard to forget about them. She felt that there was a place within her heart where she kept her favorite memories. You know -- the ones that never fail to make you smile. And when life became too hectic, it was such a special feeling to be able to just close her eyes and reminisce awhile. During her reminiscing, she sometimes wondered what it would have been like to have had brothers. She wondered if brothers would have fought a lot with her and if they would have loved her.

The ringing phone broke Melina's reverie. When she answered the phone, the familiar, sweet sounding voice on the other end almost caused her to drop it.

"Hello big sis – how are you doing? It's been a while hasn't it?" the voice said softly.

"Dannie – is this really you? But – I – I can't believe you are calling me. It's been a long time since I had heard your voice. I – I'm doing okay – especially now that I am talking to you."

"Lina, I'm so sorry I had not been in touch with you for so long, but I want to change that now. I miss you and want to try to make our relationship work. I want my big sister back in my life. Do you think that you can give me another chance?"

These words were like sweet music to Melina's ears for she had longed to have her little sister back in her life. Now it seemed that her dreams had come true. She had tried to keep the communication open between Danielle and her and had been willing to do whatever it took to try to make their relationship work.

"Of course you can have another chance Dannie. I love you and have missed having you in my life."

"That's great Lina – you won't regret it. I was hoping that you would say yes. I didn't know if you hated me or despised me or something. I know that I had been mean to you and I wanted a chance to make amends."

"I could never hate you because you are my sister. It is true that you did do some pretty hateful things to me and it hurt, but I forgive you. I'm just happy to have a chance to have a sisterly relationship with you."

"I know sis – and we will. I'd like to come and see you next weekend if it is okay with you and maybe stay for a while."

"Sure – that would be great. I will be looking forward to your arrival. Nikki is going to be so surprised by this news."

"How old is my niece now Lina?"

"She is sixteen and such a wonderful girl. I'm so proud of her."

"Okay sis, I will be looking forward to seeing all of you next weekend, okay? Bye sis."

Melina was still standing there holding the phone in her hands even though Danielle had hung up. She was in shock from the realization of hearing from her sister after all this time. Placing the phone back into its cradle, Melina walked back to kitchen table and sat down. Her eyes fell on an album page that had a ten year old photo of Dannie. Her eyes welled with tears as she remembered that just moments earlier she had wished that she had her little sister back in her life. Now she will have another chance to be close with her younger sibling again. She felt strongly that the two of them could work through their differences if both of them worked at it and wanted it. Melina thought, that to every action there is a reaction. The experience may be the same, but what needs to change is how she had experienced the experience. If she asked God and the Holy Spirit to change the way she had perceived her sister's anger and hatred towards her, to change or shift her reaction to her outbursts, then she may be very surprised, as will Danielle. She thought that maybe Dannie had been lashing out against her because maybe she somehow had felt inferior, and the only way she feel good was to make her feel poorly. Maybe Danielle was in some type of deep inward pain. Maybe there was something very important missing in her life, which was probably why she was always angry with me, scheming, etc.. Maybe Danielle was searching and grabbing for materials things, not knowing that it will not fulfill her any further than she is now. So she decided to pray for her sister, and for herself. She asked God to bring peace to her Dannie's life, and in doing so, maybe it will bring peace to hers. Melina had to ask herself whether she wanted to be right, or be happy. She wanted to be happy so she was ready to look beyond her sister's angry reminders and she was able, she thought, to forgive her sister for turning their adult years into one explosion after another. Melina felt she was ready to move on and become real sisters with Danielle again.

Chapter

Seven

"*Okay, I'm awake*," Melina said groggily, sitting up and allowing a huge yawn to escape. Satisfied with her acknowledgement of the new day, the sun dispersed its reflection, leaving her to rub her stunned eyes. Though she wanted to move the mirror, the glare served as a useful alarm clock. Sitting up in bed, she pushed herself up and walked over to the large mirror on her dresser, talking to the reflection as to a familiar friend. *"Did you ever believe that your little sister would be coming to visit you?"* Not waiting for a reply, she continued, *"I'm so glad that she is coming!* Her face saddened a little as she stared at an old scar on her cheek where Dannie had scratched her several years back when she had gotten physical with her. The one-inch scar was a negative reminder of how violent her sister could be when she was angered. But now Melina was looking forward to major changes in her life. She had a brighter future within her grasp now that Dannie was coming back into her life. She was almost afraid to entertain the thought of the possibility that she and Danielle may be able to mend the rift between them. The chance to have a real relationship with her younger sister was within her grasp and it felt wonderful.

The week seemed to drag on endlessly. Melina was really looking forward to this weekend – to be able to see her sister again and try to work through the problems they have had over the years. This meeting was something that she thought she would never see, yet now it seems to be becoming a reality.

It was Wednesday evening and Melina had just gotten home from work. She changed into a pair of sweats, poured her a half a glass of chardonnay, and plopped down in her recliner. All she wanted was to unwind from the very hectic busy day she had endured. Her eyes fell upon her photo album that she left on the end table from the day before. She got up, collected the album, and returned to her chair. Melina slowly turned the pages and admired the photos of her family and past life with her sister Dannie. Tears teased the corners of her eyes as she paused on a photo of her parents. Both are deceased now. Her father had passed on years ago and her mother had died almost two years back. Outside of her immediate family, her mother had been the only person she had talked to about Danielle. Her mother had always tried to discourage her from trying to re-connect with her younger sister. *That damn Danielle is a lost cause and to just leave her be. You better off without her child – the girl is crazy as a loon and disrespectful. I tried to raise her right just as I did with you but she just was hard-headed and disobedient. I say the hell with her and let God deal with her,* were the words of their mother echoing through her mind.

Melina continued turning the pages of the album until she ran across a picture of her and Danielle. Three years separated their ages but you would have thought differently if you saw how Dannie dressed and acted – always trying to act as though she was so much older than me.

Melina's mind visited a time in high school when Danielle had been flirting with her boyfriend Kevin and they had gotten into a huge fight. Dannie had vowed that she would get even with me because I had gotten the best of her in the fight. One night, Melina had stopped by her boyfriend's house to return some history notes and he didn't answer the door after several knocks. She knew he was at home because his car was parked in the driveway, but thought that maybe he had fallen asleep. She went around the house to his bedroom window to knock again and hoped that he would hear her. A light was on in his room but he still didn't acknowledge hearing her knocks on the window. After hearing a noise in his room, Melina noticed a small opening between the curtain and the window and decided to try to look inside. When she peeked through the opening, she could believe what she was seeing -- Kevin was making out with Danielle. She was in such shock and just couldn't believe that her boyfriend was cheating on her with her own sister. Melina became furious and was very hurt by the betrayal of her sister and Kevin. Suddenly, she remembered that Dannie was a minor and that this shit was going to be stopped right now. She ran two houses down the street to her cousin Troy's house to enlist his help in getting into Kevin's house. When she and Troy returned to the house, he kicked the door in and both of them went inside. Melina retrieved her sister and Troy hit Kevin several times and warned him to stay away from both his cousins or he would be sorry. And Melina threatened that if he told anyone about who kicked the door in on his house that he would be turned in for statutory rape because Danielle was only 14 years old.

After Melina and Danielle returned home, her little sister was still defiant and hostile toward her. Melina asked Dannie how she could have done something so low as sleeping with her boyfriend Kevin. The only answer she gave her was that she had warned her when they last fought that she would get even. Danielle had over-heard her sister Melina say that she would be going by Kevin's house, so she timed it so that her older sister would find her there having sex with her boyfriend.

Danielle taunted Melina about how Kevin liked her better and that she couldn't compete with her. She continued with her insults and sarcastic words until Melina became so angry that she screamed at her. *"Why you stupid little whore – this is not a competition and I am not trying to compete with you. You just gave your body up to that no good son-of-a-bitch for nothing. Kevin ain't shit if he would sleep with my sister and you ain't shit for letting him fuck you. The only thing that you and Kevin managed to do was prove was that neither one of you have any morals nor respect for yourself or anyone else. You are a trifling ass little bitch that's too stupid to see when you have gone too far with this brainless bullshit of trying to hurt me."*

Momentarily there was only silence as the two sisters stood and stared at each other. Melina couldn't believe that she had just done that. It was like an out-of-body experience where she was standing outside of her own body watching someone else say all those things to her little sister.

When Danielle finally spoke, she told Melina how much she hated her and then she ran crying to her room leaving Melina feeling like shit. This episode was just one of many fights she and Dannie had during their teenage years. But their fights seemed to intensify as they grew older. But on Danielle's part, the fights had been turning more vicious and seemed to be approaching borderline sibling abuse.

Melina's relationship with her sister had gotten on a downward spiral and their connection was lost. For the next sixteen years, the two sisters' conversations were practically non-existent. There was so much bitterness that stood between them, but Melina still didn't want to accept the fact that her sister Danielle's anger, resentment, and hostility would probably not change unless it was for the worst.

Melina had discussed her sister Danielle's upcoming visit with her husband Grant and her daughter Nikki. Grant was happy for his wife as was Nikki because they both were aware of how long she had longed to have her little sister back in her life. But there was love lost between him and Danielle. He still remembered how he had allowed himself to get caught up in her immoral corruptness long ago. As far as he was concerned he didn't care if he ever saw her again. All he wanted to do now was support his wife. Melina's family had always been supportive of her and had agreed whole-heartedly about Danielle's visit.

Chapter

Eight

It was Saturday and it was such a wonderful and special day for Melina. In a few hours her sister Danielle would be arriving. Finally she thought, *I will have my sister back in my life and the two of us will become close as sisters should – do things together – have holiday dinners – go shopping – and just hang out. I will finally have a real sister again.*

Melina walked over to her bay window and observed the morning joggers as they ran the trail around the small lake that was the focal attraction in the park. She had many new and unfamiliar feelings stirring inside her.

The whole sister thing would be unchartered territory for her because she had never had a close relationship with Danielle. Melina understood the concept of sisterhood, but had not experienced it personally. Dannie had made sure that from an earlier age up until just recently, that her big sister would know about nothing except how much she had despised her.

There had been so much animosity between Melina and Danielle that it had felt as though a reunion or re-connection seemed nearly impossible and hopeless. Their adult sibling rivalry had started out from childhood sibling rivalry - but they are two very different types of family conflict. Fighting with a grown sister is quite different than childhood conflict. When they were children, their childhood conflicts was suppose to teach them how to relate to others -- sometimes for good, sometimes for bad. Either way, their adult relationships were definitely affected by this rivalry. When you're struggling with adult sibling rivalry, your experiences can change how you communicate with your partner or children. Melina's earlier relationship with her husband Grant had some remnants of the affects her estranged sister's actions had set into motion years ago but Melina never really knew the true essence of the situation. She had no idea to how close to home her little sister's dealings really reached, but Danielle and Grant do.

Melina had recognized that many of the problems she'd had with Grant stemmed from her unresolved childhood conflicts, but worked diligently to keep her marriage intact. Melina and Danielle's parent's attempt to treat both of them equally may had been in vain because picking a favorite would have been evolutionary. Many parents are programmed to spend the most time and energy on the sibling that seems most worthy of investment because there is a finite supply of love, affection, money, and security. As a child Melina initially had believed her parents loved both of them the same. Her parents seemed to have a primal mindset to put more effort into the smart, gifted, attractive kid.

Melina had remembered a study she had read in a magazine that concluded that 70% of fathers and 65% of mothers show a preference for one child – usually, the older one. And the kids know it, which feeds both child and adult sibling rivalry. She tried to educate herself as much as possible about the conflicts he'd had with her sister so that she could try to understand what she had been going through. Melina strong determination and the love of her family would not allow her to give up. She learned that childhood sibling rivalry didn't automatically doom her to failure or set her up for success - and neither will this adult sibling rivalry with her sister Dannie. Other aspects of her life and personality were just as important, such as how she dealt with failure, what tickled her funny bone, and even her propensity towards depression. She just wasn't going to let it beat her.

"Mom always did like you best!" were the words Danielle had hurled in Melina's face countless times in her life. These words and many others Danielle had said made her sad, but she tried not to dwell on it. Instead, Melina had found ways of dealing with the raw feelings, the hurt, and the stress from her ordeal. She chose to try not taking it personally, found support elsewhere in her life, trying not to perpetuate sibling rivalry, learned to accept the reality of the situation, and invested in her own family. Melina knew she had a committed relationship and a family of her own, so she chose to focus on providing that which she had wished she had gotten from her sister. She chose to focus on what she shared with them, and on what she provided to herself in life. By doing all of these things, she would be better able to accept the familiar quirks of her sister.

Melina tried to dismiss those hurtful thoughts of Danielle's past aggressions from her mind so that she could focus on her little sister's arrival, but the thoughts kept returning as if it they were some kind of omen. Melina began making preparations for Dannie's arrival. In a couple of days, she would be here and they to work on being real sisters again.

Familiar arms encircling her waist broke her silent thoughts of her sister.

"Good morning Mama," Nikki said, resting her head on the back of my neck.

"Good morning sweetie. Are you ready to see your aunt Danielle?"

"I guess so Mama – don't remember much about her though."

"Well baby that will change now that she's coming here to visit for a while. You look happy Nikki."

"I'm happy that you are happy Mama. I know how much you have wanted this reunion and it has been a long time coming."

"Yes -- I am very happy and excited about my little sister being here."

"Hey – let's break up this hugging stuff in here and give me a chance to get one," Grant said, entering the den.

"Hi Daddy – how are you this morning?" Nikki said, after walking over to her father and kissing him on the cheek.

"I'm good baby girl," her father replied with a wink.

The doorbell rang out. When Melina opened the door, there stood Danielle smiling broadly.

"Dannie! Dannie!" Melina cried out, throwing her arms around Danielle.

The two of them broke their embrace and looked at each other momentarily.

"Hello Sis, long time no see," Danielle finally said.

"I am so happy that you are here Danielle – we all are," Melina said, grabbing her little sister's hand and leading her inside. Melina asked Grant and Nikki to get her sister's luggage as the two sisters continued on inside to the den.

Melina, Danielle, Grant and Nikki all gathered in the den. Danielle knew them all by name but really didn't know much else about them. Now it was time for Dannie to get acquainted with her new family.

Chapter

Nine

Danielle had been living at Melina's home for about a month and decided that it was time to commence with phase two of her plan to destroy her sister. As hard as it had been for her to play nice with her sister, Dannie knew that the day would eventually come that she would be able to topple Melina's world.

Melina had her sisters' room fixed up very nicely because she took pride in being able to offer her sister the best of things. She believed that nothing was too good for little sister Danielle and she was thrilled to have her in her life again.

When Dannie arose that Saturday morning, she pretended to want to be close to her niece Nikki – which was part of her plan to hurt her sister Melina. Dannie had dressed and went into the kitchen to make breakfast. Melina and Grant both had gone to work and she figured this would be the opportune time to start to work on Nikki. As she was finishing preparing breakfast, Nikki entered the kitchen.

"Something sure smells good aunt Dannie," she said smiling, seating herself on a barstool in the kitchen.

"Good morning Nikki. I thought we might eat breakfast and go shopping today. It will be my treat."

"Really? I would love to go shopping."

"I never got a chance to spoil you when you were growing up, but I can make up for it now. You will be going off to college in about six months and I know you will need some hip clothes," Danielle said, placing their plates on the table. "Come on over here girl and eat up. We will have a busy day today."

Danielle and Nikki seated themselves at the table and began eating. As Danielle ate, she gazed at Nikki occasionally with contempt in her eyes. Nikki had not noticed a thing and was engrossed in eating and chattering about shopping. Danielle thought to herself, *this stupid, pathetic little shit thinks I care about her but I don't. I don't give a damn about her or her mother. Both of them are just a means to an end. They are only objects – they are just things in my way. I will show them who the better woman is. Melina thinks she has the world in a bottle with the stopper in her hands just because she got married and had a child. She doesn't have a better job than I do and doesn't make better money than me. Soon and very soon she will be just like me – alone and without a mate because she doesn't deserve it. I will take away all that she hold dear and then I will be the best woman.*

"Aunt Dannie, I know some great boutiques here that we can go to today," Nikki said, invading Danielle's wicked thoughts.

"Okay Nikki," Danielle replied with a mischievous grin. "We can get started as soon as we're finished with breakfast."

After breakfast, Danielle and Nikki did the dishes together. Danielle washed the dishes while Nikki dried them. Very soon afterward, they were on their way shopping.

Danielle and Nikki's first stop was to the Westfield Gateway Mall. This mall was the oldest of the two (the other is South Pointe Mall) and is located just east of downtown. The anchors were Sears, Dillard's, Younkers and JCPenney and over 120 other stores including Buckle, Finish Line, New York & Company, Victoria's Secret, etc. Though not a glamorous upscale mall, it did have a running carousel like Southridge Mall in Des Moines, Iowa and Coral Ridge Mall in Coralville (Iowa City)

Iowa), it had some decent restaurants surrounding the mall such as Granite City and Olive Garden along with a decent food court and an Applebee's.

Danielle and Nikki's second stop was the Nebraska's Centennial Mall. The mall served as the scenic connection between the Nebraska's iconic State Capitol and the University of Nebraska-Lincoln. The mall's many fountains had been a source of pride for many Nebraskans and were featured in a variety of the state's tourism and promotional materials. This mall had been built in 1967 to commemorate the state's centennial year, Centennial Mall extends from the State Capitol seven blocks north on what would be 15th Street and is part of the City Parks system.

Nikki and Danielle's last stop was the Southpointe Pavilions Mall. They saved this mall for last because this was would be where they would eat. The SouthPointe Pavilions is a Williamsburg-style lifestyle center featuring six popular anchor tenants blended with more than 40 upscale shops, and a 6-plex movie theatre. Their restaurants included Carlos O'Kelly's, Chili's, Cold Stone Creamery, Famous Dave's, The Food Court, Macaroni Grill, McDonald's, Old Chicago, Panera Bread, and Taco Bell just to name a few. The mall also had many specialty stores such as Barnes and Noble, Bath & Body Works, Beauty First, Claire's Accessories, Francesca's Collections, The Face Place Spa, and Victoria's Secret.

When Nikki and Danielle finished their shopping, they headed for Old Chicago to eat their fill of real, Chicago-style pizza. This restaurant also made great calzones, burgers, and salads.

After eating so much pizza, Nikki and Danielle thought that it would be a good idea to walk some of it off. Danielle and Nikki stopped by the Sunken Gardens at 27th and Capital Parkway. As the only Nebraska garden listed in the "300 Best Gardens to Visit in the United States and Canada" by National Geographic Guide to Public Gardens, this was a special place to many. Visitors could tiptoe through the tulips every spring and watch the thousands of annuals bloom all summer long. Nikki and Danielle strolled through the beautiful gardens and chatted about their shopping experience.

The Sunken Garden had three other gardens inside it. The garden features were The Healing Garden (or White Garden) which was located in the upper level on the west side. The design was inspired by the famous White Garden at Sissinghurst Castle in Kent, England created in the 1930's by Vita Sackville West and Harold Nicholson. The gathering of white blossoms inspires calm, serenity and recreation. Visitors were encouraged to experience the ethereal quality of the garden on moonlit summer evenings. Then there was the Perennial Garden located throughout Sunken Gardens but was featured in the upper level on the north side. There they saw varieties of hosta, viburnum and hydrangea – an inspiration for design elements in others areas of the garden. And last but not least, they walked through the Annual Garden. Thousands of annuals were planted, many by volunteers, corresponding to a different theme each spring. Primarily serving as design inspiration, garden themes have included Americana, Van Gogh's "Starry Night", Hachimaki – a stylized Japanese headband.

After the trip to the Sunken Garden, Danielle and Nikki left for home. They both were pleased with their purchases and Danielle had actually enjoyed the outing with her niece. But she would never let her niece know the two truths about today – the trip was planned as a part of her revenge plot and the other truth being that she really did enjoy the time spent with Nikki shopping. After today, Danielle realized that she was going to have to work harder to not become too close to her niece in fear that she could foil her plans. She knew she had to keep her eye on the prize.

Chapter

Ten

Danielle continues with her wicked plans of destroying her sister Melina's life. When she awoke this morning, a pleased feeling washed over her. Her clear-cut plans seemed to be taking shape. She was counting the days until she was able to tell Melina just how pathetic and stupid she had been for believing that she actually wanted a real sisterly relationship with her.

Danielle's mind visited a time in her past when she had done something really low down to her sister Melina. She basked in the thought of her act as if it were a major, grand accomplishment. Danielle smiled contently thinking of how she had betrayed her sister back then. This misdeed happened during the time of their father's funeral and to this day Melina knows nothing of it. Danielle had had sex with Grant in the bathroom of their parents' home while her family and family friends dined in the foyer. She enjoyed living her life on the edge and the mere thought that she and Grant could be discovered at any time excited her. She giggled to herself as she remembered how embarrassed Grant was afterward. Just before he walked out of the bathroom, he turned to her, grabbed her by both shoulders firmly, and looking square in the eyes. He told her that this despicable act could never ever happen again because he her loved Melina. He warned Danielle to never speak of their indiscretion - NEVER. He stormed out of the back door furious with himself for what he had just done with his sister-in-law-to-be.

Soft knocking on her the bedroom door interrupted her daydream.

"Come on in," Danielle spoke.

It was her sister Melina carrying a breakfast tray.

"I thought that maybe you would like some breakfast little sister."

"Lina – you didn't have to go to the trouble of cooking me breakfast."

"I really didn't mind at all Danny. You know how I enjoy cooking. I thought that maybe we could chat and catch up some. And afterward, we might be able to go shopping or something."

"I would like that sis. After all, I want to spend as much quality time with you as possible. Getting to know my family again is all I want. You know – we could go to the mall and have facials, manicures, pedicures, and massages. And it would all be my treat to you Lina for being so forgiving and understanding. You are allowing me back into your life and I want to so my appreciation for that generosity."

"That is a great idea Danny. I would like for us to have time together and do things together like normal sisters do. I'm so grateful to have you back in my life."

"I'm going to finish breakfast, shower and dress. And maybe we could leave in about an hour?" Danielle suggested.

"Sounds good to me Danny," Melina said smiling warmly.

After Melina walked out and closed the door, Danielle stuck her finger in her mouth as if you would gag and then rolled her eyes. She thought to herself, stupid, stupid Melina. If you only knew – I could care less about getting close to you. I can't stand you. I despise you – you b.i.t.c.h -- and you will know just how much I hate you before this is all over. I'm going to make your husband sleep with me again and I will have the satisfaction of throwing that indiscretion in your sanctimonious face.

An hour and twenty minutes later, Melina and Danielle arrived at Tranquility Spa & Salon. It was conveniently located across from Southpointe Mall in Lincoln, Nebraska. This establishment offered a wide variety of services such as hair, nails, facials, massage body treatment, hair removal, and tanning. They also had spa packages and wedding packages.

"Wow Danielle – this place is beautiful," Melina said in amazement.

This type of environment was a familiar scene for Danielle because she had always treated herself to the luxury of being pampered. She felt that she had never gotten that type of treatment when she was growing up because of their mother always favored her older sibling Melina. After reaching adulthood, Danielle vowed to always pamper herself and the hell with everyone else.

"Yeah it is a pretty fly place Lina. What do you want to try first?"

"I've never had a professional spa treatment so what about doing that first?"

"Sure sis – it's whatever you want today – my treat remember?"

Danielle and Melina headed for the spa. Danielle chose the five and half hour Spa Indulgence package which included a signature facial, a full body Swedish massage, a spa manicure, a spa pedicure with moisture masque, a nano luxury deep conditioning treatment and style, and make-up application.

This salon offered a lot of body and massage treatments. There was the Swedish massage that was designed to relax tired muscles and increase circulation. It also helped to reduce stress and promoted a sense of well-being and is recommended for those that have never had a massage. The Aromatherapy massage was a luxurious full body massage using essential oils to stimulate the skin and senses and it was the ultimate massage experience for balancing of the mind, body, and spirit. The Deep Tissue Massage was therapeutic and catered to specific muscle tension areas. This would be the perfect massage to have to help ease muscle tightness and tired joints that have been over used during rigorous exercise.

After Danielle and Melina were finished with their luxurious spa, manicure and pedicure treatments, eating was next on the list of things-to-do. The two of them decided on eating at Romano's Macaroni Grill. Romano's Macaroni Grill is a casually elegant Italian restaurant serving handcrafted pastas, craveable entrees, and a diverse wine list. This restaurant boasted 20 years of tradition with innovative Italian cooking and it also provided a rich experience that could only be matched by its delicious food. The quality Italian ingredients, honor system wine and opera singers showcase the restaurant's heritage, while your table top masterpieces and wine bottle murals bring new energy to every meal. The fresh pastas, regional ingredients and diverse wine list boast of what's to come, yet the classics and traditions continue to tempt. The atmosphere wasn't intimidating and was very comfortable and it delivered an experience that was perfect to celebrate their big day.

Melina and Danielle made their selection from the Principale Menu and both selected Florentine Steak & Frites prime sirloin, arugula pesto, parmesan fries and a Caesar salad. The ladies desired a smooth, tasty wine to compliment their meal, so the wine waiter suggested that the Gainey Merlot may be more to their liking. The wine waiter had told them that this merlot wine had a shimmering ruby color; it has enticingly fresh, vivid aromas of black cherry and red plum fruit, perfectly complemented by fragrant rose hips tea, sweet oak and light herbal tones. In the mouth, the flavors were startlingly rich, creamy and luscious, with concentrated red cherry and plum skin fruitiness invigorated by seeped-tea spice tones and tangy acidity. Those who can't wait are advised to uncork this beauty with herb-roasted chicken, black-olive pizza or Merlot-marinated game hen.

Melina and Danielle learned that the Gainey Merlot turned out to be a very great tasting Merlot just as the waiter said. With 15% Cabernet Franc, it added a welcome cherry tart richness to the earthy blackberries and herbs. This Merlot was priced well for an elegant restaurant wine and it was dry, crisp and smooth, and so easy to drink with their fine steaks.

The two sisters ate and enjoyed their meals before returning to the house. Danielle had purchased an extra bottle of wine to take home with them. When they arrived, Nikki and Grant were not there yet. Melina decided to take this opportunity to chat alone with her little sister without any interruptions.

"Dannie – I have wanted to ask you something since you've been here but I didn't want to ask in front of Nikki or Grant."

"What is it Lina – ask away. I have nothing to hide."

"How often did you think of me over the years?

"I thought of you often Lina I was just so ashamed of how I had acted and treated you. I didn't know how to ask for your forgiveness."

"You know Dannie – I had forgiven you years ago because I just couldn't hold all of that hostility against you. It hurt to try to keep so much hurtful stuff inside and I also missed you terribly in my life. It was my daily prayer to have you come back into my life so that we could try to be close sisters and move forward. I never understood where all of your anger toward me came from and why you had done so many cruel things to me."

"Lina – I am sorry for the hurt and the cruel acts that I committed toward you. I think it had a lot to do with our mother. She seemed to favor you over me and she would always say to me, why can't you be more like your sister Melina? She compared everything I did to you."

Danielle paused momentarily and her eyes became watery. She composed herself and then she continued.

"I felt like I grew up in your shadow – always wanting to measure up to what our mother thought that I should be. I didn't know how to deal with it so I took it out on you."

"I am so sorry that you felt that our mother picked favorites because I had believed that she loved us both the same. I can't take away the pain for the years you suffered with those thoughts but we can start here now and create new happy, loving, and compassionate ones. I love you Dannie – I always have."

Melina and Danielle came together and hugged. All seemed right for the two sisters in their world. Melina felt in her heart at that moment that things would be staying that way.

Chapter

Eleven

After Melina and Danielle's heart-to-heart talk, Danielle felt secure in her mind that she had her big sister in the right mindset to continue her manipulation of her. When she thought of the words that her sister caused her to have to say during their momentous sister bonding moment, Danielle became angry. It took all that was within her to try to past off sincerity when she spoke to Melina. But within moments her anger dissipated and was replaced by an impish grin. She now was feeling much gratification in fact that Nikki had really taken to her. Danielle also believed that she now didn't have to work on her so hard to totally gain her trust. She had Nikki eating out of the palms of her hands.

As for Grant, Danielle knew that he would be a bit harder to sway. He practically hated her because of her manipulative ways. But she believes in her feminine charm and is confident that she can get Grant to sleep with her again. If she could just get pregnant by him she knows that this would be the almost the ultimate betrayal. Grant is just a man and he can be enticed just like any other man according to her play book.

Danielle had done some research on determining when a woman is most fertile. There is only a limited amount of time when a woman can get pregnant every month. While the fertility window does vary from woman to woman, most women are fertile for about five to seven days each month. Even so, it can often take up to a year to become pregnant once you begin trying. She knew that she needed to figure out when she would be ovulating in order to determine the best time to get pregnant. Danielle tracked her menstrual cycle and used an ovulation calculator_to determine her ovulation window, she observed her vaginal discharge, took her temperature every morning, before she get out of bed, and purchased a home ovulation predictor kit. After keeping track of everything for a month, Danielle determined that tonight would be the night to try to conceive a baby with Grant.

A sinfully impious smile crept over Danielle's face as she thought of how naïve her sister Melina had been in believing that she wanted anything to do with her, let alone to reconnect with her. Winning Melina's trust would not be an issue because she knew how much her older sister wanted a close relationship with her. This closeness – this sisterly bonding that Melina wants so much is what she will use against her – it will be her sister's downfall. Danielle knows that she won't have to make much of an effort to get Melina to believe in her. Her plan will go off without a hitch and Melina will never know what hit her until it is too late – and then Danielle will have her ultimate revenge on her big sister.

Danielle needs to execute her plan of seduction on Grant as soon as possible. She has been in her sister Melina's home long enough now to learn everyone's schedule. Nikki spends the night with her friend Xandria on Thursday nights. Melina works the night shift at her job this week and Grant will be home by 8 p.m. nightly unless he was working out of town. Having this knowledge Danielle knew that this really was the best night to commence with her plan to seduce Grant because would be at home alone tonight. All she had to do was to wait until Grant had gotten into bed and had fallen asleep before putting her plan in action.

Danielle patiently waited until she was sure Grant was asleep. The bedroom was dark as she entered and she could barely see except for the light that protruded from a small crack in the bathroom door. When she reached the bed, she undressed allowing her panties and bra to drop to the floor. Then she slid underneath the covers next to Grant snuggling as close as she could possibly get to him. Reaching over him she located and began massaging his member. Grant began to respond to her touch releasing deep, rasping moans of pleasure. Clasping her hands in his he copied the motion she had begun moments earlier, stroking and massaging his now stiffened manhood. With his eyes still closed, he turned to her pulling her up to him while laying claim to one of her plump, soft breasts.

A soft moan fell from Danielle's lips as she tried hard to remain quiet during this experience. She did not want to let on to Grant that she was not Melina yet and she also wanted to continue with this sexual encounter.

Grant quickly removes his pajama bottoms and continues ravaging Danielle's body. His roaming hand soon finds her moist treasure box as his fingers gently massages her silk button. Sighs of exquisite pleasure began to run rapacious through her body until she could barely contain them. Grant was sending her entire body into such a fevered frenzy that when he slowly entered her, she bit her lip to try to prevent the overwhelming sounds of pleasure that were about to escape her lips. Grant's lovemaking had become so intense that she could no longer be quiet and had to release herself.

"Oh Grant, this feels so good baby, yes – yes—yes-s-s-s-s-s," she cried out.

That very instant Grant stopped because he couldn't believe what he had just heard. He leaned over to the night stand and turned on the lamp. What he saw almost sent him into shock. He hastily jumped from the bed and yelled at Danielle.

"Danielle --- what the hell do you think you are doing? Why the hell are you in my bed? How did you – why are you – dam it Danielle – this is your sister's bed. How could you do – you made me make love – I can't believe I made love to you -- and in my wife's bed."

"Grant!" Danielle called out.

"I got to find my clothes." Grant muttered. "Where is my underwear"

"Grant!"

"I can't believe this has happened -- again. I can't believe this shit."

"Grant!" Danielle yelled.

"What!" he yelled back angrily. "Get the hell out of my bed you trashy little bitch. This is your fault. Why would you come here and do some fucked up shit like this?"

Grant fumbled about until he put his underwear on, plopped down on the side of the bed, and dropped his head into his hands. "I just can't believe this shit." He said rocking back and forth. "How did I let you do this to me again? I have really fucked up this time."

"Yeah you did fuck up Grant – and in the worst possible way," Danielle said sitting up in bed and smiling contently.

"It was as good as I remembered and I just couldn't keep quiet any longer. Why don't you come on back to bed for round two?" she teased.

Grant lifted his head and gazed at Danielle with the evil eye. "Are you crazy? I would have never made love to you again if I had known that was you. You are the most manipulative, scheming, foolish-ass woman I have ever seen. I didn't want your ass back then and I sure as hell don't want you now."

Danielle got out of bed and walked around it to where Grant was sitting and grabbed a hold of his manhood again, shoving him down on the bed. She knew just how to work a man and Grant was no exception. She would get what she wanted one way or another.

"Danielle – you get off me right now and stop this shit." Grant raved.

Danielle ignored his words and continued her quest of seduction. She suddenly kissed him and which led to kissing him deeper and deeper. Grant pushed her away but she returned with an even more aggressive kiss. This time Grant didn't fight as hard against her and his love muscle had begun hardening once again. She stroked his rod of pleasure quickly; bringing it to its full state of hardness.

"Danielle – we – we – can't do this. This – this – is wrong. Please – don't. Don't. We can't do this again," Grant begged with his resistance depleted.

"Do you want me to stop baby?" she said, placing his erect member between her full lips.

Danielle began sliding his member in and out of her mouth, pausing briefly to massage it. Danielle was skilled at oral sex and would not stop no matter what Grant said. It was becoming clear to her that Grant didn't want her to stop anyway because he had begun moaning and groaning and his voice had become raspy.

"Danielle – I – I – love Melina. I – I – promised to never let – let – this – happen again. Dan –ielle – this is – immoral – and disrespectful to your sis – ter."

"But you know you like this baby – you know Dannie know how to please her man. You know my stuff is good too don't you baby – don't you? You know that I know how to work it."

Danielle began pulling on it gently trying to make him move so that she could slide herself onto it. He got the message, moving his hips slowly toward her as she moved her legs around him. She made him stay on his back as she mounted him sliding all the way down his now vertical manhood. She placed her hands on his chest giving out a heavy sigh as inch by inch he filled her tight *velvet love-canal*. She smiled down at him giving her hips a little flip and he moaned feeling his member move slightly while inside her. She began to slide up now quickly forcing herself back down once she reached the top of him. Grant closed his eyes, seeing stars from where she had just made his member re-enter her love box with such a hard stroke. He moaned softly and Danielle just smiled sliding nearly all the way off of him before taking all of his manhood back into her fiery furnace again.

Grant's hands went to cup her breasts as he squeezed them gently; massaging them between his index and thumbs and coming up to rub at her nipples as he massaged them. Danielle began lengthening her strokes taking him fully at the end of every one and quickly Grant could hold back no longer as he started to shoot into her hard, timing it just right as she shot off into an orgasm of her own. The two of them lay as still as possible trying to let the tremors wear off some.

Grant had other ideas though, lifting Danielle off of him as he then took his semi-hard member in his hands pointing it at her lips as if to taunt her. She was more than happy to take him into her mouth though, as she began sucking gently. She massaged his balls helping him to moan and he had trouble getting her to release him before he had another blast off but he got her to lie on her stomach as he rubbed his manhood all over the cheeks of her buttocks, savoring the feel of her delicate skin. She quickly rose to her knees, stretching out on all fours as

Grant smiled moving his hips so that he was now lined up with her once again dripping tunnel of love.

Grant placed his hands on her shoulders shoving his hips forward brutally burying his length into her as she moaned hard and loud but that didn't deter him from continuing his onslaught. He took five more straight strokes deep into her before giving her a second to rest as he moved his hands down massaging her breasts gently rubbing over her nipples again.

Once again he started the fire in her and before long she was bucking her hips back at him, Grant allowed her to, watching her ass move back and forth then suddenly he leveled her right buttock with a hard slap as she stopped moving immediately almost crying out from the pain of the smack. He then took another thrust into her that was twice as hard as Danielle lay forward holding her ass up to him for his taking. Grant smiled at her, realizing that he had her now where he wanted her, on her hands and knees begging for him to fuck her.

He now quickened his pace and the strength of his thrusts as he felt himself begin to cum he felt her velvet glove squeezing down on him tightly as they each reached their climax together.

Afterward, when he had a little time to relax and reality had a chance to sink in, Grant felt horrible for the act he had just committed with is sister-in-law Danielle. He got up from the bed and walked over to photo of he and Melina hanging on the wall. As he stared at the picture, he questioned how he could have done such a thing to his wife. He had just made love to his wife's sister in their bed and in the home he and his wife had happily sustained for the nearly eighteen years. To him his actions with Danielle were the lowest of the low deeds that a man could do and he – Grant Harrington, had just done it. The guilt and betrayal made him angry with Danielle and himself. He rushed back over to the bed where Danielle lay dozing and shook her briskly.

"Get up Danielle – get up!

Danielle sits up in the bed and groggily looks up at Grant.

"What! What's the problem?" she asks showing no remorse or concern for what had just happened between her and Grant.

"You know you are a real piece of work. How could you come here and get me sucked back into this thing with you? After all these years I thought I had built up a resistance against you. I find myself drawn to you physically and I can't seem to help it regardless of how I try to fight it. But see what's going on here. You are here to hurt your sister – but why? Haven't you hurt her enough over the years? You know – she loves you but you don't want to see that do you?"

Danielle turns her head away as Grant speaks solemnly about her sister Melina. She did not want to hear this stuff because it wouldn't change anything.

"Grant I don't want to hear this."

"The only thing that your sister wanted was to have a normal relationship with you – to be a sister. I used to try to encourage her to forget about you – to just write you off. But she wouldn't do it. And after seeing how much not having you in her life was hurting her, I changed my mind. I thought that maybe – just maybe you had changed. So I began supporting her in everything she wanted because I wanted to see her happy. When she told me that you were coming to visit, I thought – wow – she may get to have her little sister back in her life after all."

Tears started to tease the corners of Danielle's eyes as she turns her head away from Grant's view. She vowed to herself that these residual feelings would be no more after this night. War has been declared and there was no turning back now.

Suddenly Danielle head snaps around, she jumps from the bed, puts her bra and panties on, and stands up to face off with Grant.

"I hate my sister and everything she stands for because she thinks she has the perfect little life here and everybody thinks she's Miss Perfect. Well Grant – you will help me carry out my plans because I know you won't hurt Melina like that. Also, you will have sex with me whenever I want too because if you don't I will make sure your that your precious Nikki finds out about us and then your wife," Danielle threatened.

"You wouldn't – I mean – you couldn't do something like that would you?"

"I can and I will if you don't do what I want. And I don't care where we have sex just as long as I get mine."

"Danielle – I don't think that I can go through with this. How can I continue this charade with you and face my wife and daughter everyday knowing I'm deceiving them both?"

"You will do it or you will have to see your daughter and Melina find out about us sleeping together."

"But you can't be that cruel Danielle."

Danielle shot Grant a serious look and said, "Try me and see – just try me okay? Now you need to change the bed linen and get some sleep because I'm going to get me some sleep."

Before leaving the room Danielle deeply kisses Grant and grabs and massages his manhood. He pushes her away as if repulsed by her actions.

"I will see you both at a TBA (time to be announced)," she said winking her eye seductively.

Grant sat on the side of the bed with his head dropped and feeling totally lost and disheveled. How could he have betrayed the woman he loves this way – especially in the bed the two of them have shared for so many years he thought? How was he going to face Melina, make love to her, and sleep next to her knowing he has done this dirty deed with her sister Danielle? He has slept with the devil and lost his own soul and can't do anything to change it. All of the regrets or anything else would change the fact that Melina will be hurt and in the worst possible way. Grant had just realized that he has been recruited to help destroy his marriage to Melina – his wonderful, loving wife.

Danielle continued her affair with Grant over the next few months and neither Melina nor Nikki suspected a thing. Her devious plans were coming off without a hitch and she was enjoying every minute of it. Each day that passed was bringing her closer and closer to her goal of destroying her sister's life.

About two months after she and Grant started their affair, Danielle finds out that she is pregnant with his child. She made sure to tell Grant about the pregnancy because she wanted him to know that she had more leverage against him in case he starts to consider confessing him and Danielle's dirty deeds to Melina. Danielle is thrilled about being pregnant because she knows what it would do to Melina when she finds out about it. And she would make sure that she found out about the pregnancy when the time was right.

Danielle was becoming too comfortable in having her way that she had started to get a little careless. Carelessness can throw a monkey wrench into the most well-laid of plans and she would reap those consequences sooner than she had planned.

Danielle and Grant had not been sleeping together much at the house and had been using hotels in the Lincoln area. On this particular day they had chosen the Embassy Suites Lincoln which was just minutes from the campus of the University of Nebraska at Lincoln. Nikki and Xandria had been visiting different colleges in the Lincoln area to see if they wanted to attend any of them after graduation. They had received letters from several colleges in Lincoln inviting them to enroll because they had scholarships and both were honor roll students.

Nikki and Xandria had visited Union College, Nebraska Wesleyan University, Hamilton College and they were on their way to the University of Nebraska Lincoln. As they drove past the Embassy Suites Hotel, Nikki saw her father and Danielle getting out of his car and walking up toward the hotel. Nikki watched on in disbelief because she knew that she really didn't see what she thought she had seen.

"What's wrong Nikki – do you see something?" Xandria asked.

"Uh-h-h - no - no. We're straight. I just thought we had gone past our turn," she replied.

"Oh, okay. This is the last stop and then we can go and get something to eat."

"Okay Xandria."

Nikki knew that after what she had just seen she would have to make sure that nothing was going on. From that day on she would monitor her aunt's whereabouts until she was confident that there was nothing going on with her.

Chapter

Twelve

Danielle was close to being two months into her pregnancy and Nikki was keeping a close watchful eye on her and her dad. On this day, Danielle had decided that she wanted to go shopping with her niece so she suggested going to the mall. Nikki agreed whole-heartedly about the shopping trip because she knew she would be able to watch her easily while she was with her. Danielle and Nikki visited many of their usual spots and ended up at one of the local eateries instead of eating at one of the malls.

"Nikki, I was reading the Daily Nebraskan yesterday and there's a place here in town that I wanted to try out called Yia Yia's. The paper gave the place a great rating. You want to try it?" Danielle asks in an up-beat tone.

"Sure Auntie, maybe it will be great. I'm willing to try it." Nikki replies enthusiastically.

Yia Yia's won the 2010 Daily Nebraskan restaurant bracket, and for good reason. Yia Yia's made pizza that put Sbarro to shame. You could order by the slice or a full pizza, and the bar had one of the largest selections of beer in Lincoln. Slices were themed by geography, the American, the Southern and the Francais, to name a few. You could find delicious cheese, meats and veggies on each slice, which came with a hunk of bread and butter. There were also vegan options that kept meals inclusive. The space itself offered a nice patio for warmer days and a spacious interior that included pool tables and large booths. Yia Yia's was great for an all-in-one group experience.

Danielle and Nikki found themselves a table in the restaurant, seated themselves, and placed their orders. They found the pizza to be great so they enjoyed their meal. Both thought that this was one of Lincoln's best places to hangout and there was more beer than you can imagine (over 250) and the pizza pies/slices that were made to order were phenomenal. The employees, the music and dim lighting with accented lights on the framed pictures throughout this beautiful place are enough to make you a regular customer once you visit. They also learned that there's no delivery at this restaurant. Both Danielle and Nikki agreed that delivery is for lazy people!

Nikki secretly observed Danielle. She wanted to quiz her aunt just to see what sort of answers that she would give her. Nikki still hoped deep down that her Aunt Dannie would not deliberately want to hurt her mother. Knowing how long her mother had been wishing to have her younger sister back in her life. She felt she had to assure that her aunt was on the level --- and that was to reconcile with her mother. Nikki loves her mother and was not about to allow her anyone to intentionally hurt her including her own father. She loves her father too, but if she learns that her father is indeed deceiving her mother, then she would support her mother.

After a little more time passes, Nikki works up the nerve to ask her Aunt Danielle some questions.

"Aunt Dannie, are you and mama doing okay?"

Danielle pauses briefly to collect herself because she felt that the question her niece had just asked her came out from left field. She observes Nikki strangely as if she was trying to look inside her and thought that was an odd question to ask.

"Of course we are Nikki. We are becoming closer and closer. I'm just thrilled that Melina has been so forgiving and understanding."

"Yeah --- that's my mama. She's always putting the needs of others before her own," Nikki replied smiling weakly.

"Why would you ask me a question like that Nikki?"

"I just was hoping that things were going well because I know that's what mama wanted. Having you back in her life means the world to her."

"I understand what you are saying Nikki. Believe me, I want your mother and I to be close too."

"Aunt Dannie, how long are you going to be able to stay?"

"I have another three and a half months because I had taken a six month extended leave."

"Oh that's great. I know mama is thrilled about that and so am I," Nikki replied, trying to sound reassuring.

"You ready to go home? I think we have both finished our meals."

"Sure Aunt Dannie. I'm ready when you are."

Nikki and Danielle went home and Nikki pretended to have some studying to do. She also added that she and Xandria were supposed to go to the movies later. Nikki had Xandria driving her around, but she could not share any information with her about monitoring her Aunt Dannie. Though the two of them have been best friends since they were in kindergarten, her snooping on Danielle had to remain a secret for now. She decided that some things you just have to keep to yourself. But Nikki did want to be certain about what she presumed to be going on between her aunt and father before even attempting to say anything to her mother.

Later Grant arrived home. Nikki heard him when he came in and went to see him. Nikki found her father in the den sitting in his recliner, legs crossed, reading the Daily Nebraskan, and holding his favorite drink he had just poured. Grant enjoyed sitting back, relaxing and enjoying the smooth taste of a Perfect Pour. He was safeguarding his manly side with this burly drink in his hand. His preference for enjoying this drink was to take the Johnnie Walker Blue Label neat in a snifter alongside a glass of ice water. He would sip the Johnnie Walker Blue Label and cleanse his palate with a sip of ice water. He also believed that a man who nursed his Perfect Pour -- holding the stem of his glass between his middle and ring finger, swirling the liquid around and taking the time to enjoy the aroma before sipping -- said loads about his personality --- that he was the type of guy who liked to take his time -- whether it making important decisions or pleasing his lady.

"Hi Daddy," Nikki said as she approached him.

"Hi there baby girl. How have your college inquiries been going?"

"Good Daddy, I'm just not sure which one I'm going to choose yet."

"Well sweetie you do still have time to decide."

"Daddy, I wanted to tell you that Xandria and I are going to the movies later and if it is alright with you she has invited me to a sleepover."

"No problem honey bunch. You are a very responsible young lady and I trust you to always do the right thing. So you and Xandria enjoy yourselves, okay?"

"Thanks Daddy," Nikki said smiling and planting a kiss on her father's cheek.

Nikki went back to her room and phoned her friend Xandria to ask her if she would come over to her house a little early. Her friend agreed and was over there within fifteen minutes. Nikki still couldn't let on to friend about her surveillance of Danielle and her father. She simply had to keep this mission of hers under wraps until she had more information.

Maintaining surveillance on her father and aunt was no simple feat for Nikki. She was only seventeen and her parents had not gotten her a car yet, and though she was very intelligent, she still was naïve to many of the ways of the world. Also, Nikki had the added complication of keeping things secret from everyone until she could figure out the situation. Being secretive would be a chore but she knew that it had to be done until she learns more about this odd seeming relationship between her father and aunt.

Nikki heard a door close and knew that her dad had left the den and had gone to his bedroom. Her parents' bedroom was on the floor level but adjacent to hers.

Nikki told her friend that she was going to go downstairs to get her family photo album. Instead, she had gone downstairs to see if her Aunt Danielle was going to come out of her room. Danielle's room was opposite her parents' bedroom and Nikki wanted to see if her aunt was going to come out of room since her father had just gone into his. Low and behold, Danielle does just that – she comes out of her room, quickly scans the surrounding area, and then slips into her father's room.

Nikki peers around the corner and watches her father's bedroom door, but within a few minutes Danielle quietly exits the room and heads toward the front door. Nikki ducks behind a tall, plush, ficus tree near the stairs and allows her aunt to walk pass without noticing her. In her haste, Danielle never notices Nikki there and rushes out the door.

Nikki hears her father's bedroom door opening moments later and she quickly and quietly bounds up the stairs and into her bedroom.

"Where's the photo album Nikki," Xandria asks.

"Mama must have moved because I couldn't find it," Nikki replied in her most convincing tone.

Nikki hears her father calling up to her.

"Nikki? Sweetheart? I'm going out for a little while. You and Xandria enjoy yourselves tonight, okay? And be careful."

"Okay Daddy, we will."

Grant walks out of the house closing the door behind him.

"Are you ready to go to the cinema Xandria?" Nikki asks.

"Sure girl if you are. Let's roll."

Nikki and Xandria left the house and were going to the cinema downtown. Suddenly Nikki asks her friend to make a detour before going to the cinema. Xandria looks over at Nikki and her brows crease with concern.

"What's going on Nik? Is something wrong?" Xandria asks with concern in her voice.

"Oh nothing is wrong. I just remembered that I needed to check on a schedule for classes. I forgot to pick up one when we were there a few days ago."

"Oh okay Nikki – no worries."

Xandria makes a right turn and the two girls are now headed down 2100 Vine Street toward the University of Nebraska-Lincoln.

"Xan – I also need another favor. I need for you to drop me off at the University and then go and pick up my jeans at the cleaners for me. Here is twenty dollars. I should be ready in about twenty minutes okay? Then we can go to the movies."

"Okay – see you in twenty Nik."

Nikki watches as Xandria rounds the corner and then she heads for the Embassy Hotel which was right next to the University. Her eyes swept over the vehicles in the parking lot row by row until she spots her father's pearl colored Denali. It was parked over in an area of the parking lot where there was not very adequate lighting, but Nikki made sure it was her father's SUV before heading to the hotel lobby.

Nikki goes to the front desk of the hotel. Luckily, the attendant had left momentarily so she was able to take a quick look at the registry. At first glance she didn't see Danielle's name. Then she remembered her mother saying that her aunt had been married someone named Shaun Mabry. Looking back at the registry Nikki notices the second name on the page was D. Mabry. This had to be her aunt using her married name. Her heart dropped because she had hoped that she would not see her aunt's name there, but there it was as plain as day.

Nikki leaves the hotel heavy-hearted and walks back over to the University parking lot and seats herself on the front steps of the office building. Her mind raced as thoughts and images of her father and Danielle invade her mind. A stray tear courses down her saddened angelic face as she thinks of the hurt and devastation her mother would feel if she knew that her husband and her sister were having an affair. Nikki thought to herself, *I have to be sure about all of this before going to my mother. This news will destroy her.*

Nikki brushes the tears away and gathers her composure just as Xandria approaches.

"You ready girl?" Xandria yells out of her car window.

"Of course I am. Let's ride," Nikki replies flashing on her best smile.

Nikki knew that she had to make certain that her father and aunt were involved. To be certain that what she has seen so far was true, Nikki knows that she will have to confront her Aunt Danielle and ask her point blank about this situation. She could see no other way in her mind to get at the truth. Nikki is also feeling that the simple truth is going to be – her father and aunt are indeed having an affair.

Chapter

Thirteen

Nikki continues with her self-appointed chore of monitoring Danielle and her father's activities. She had been observing the two of them for over a month and had been successful in being undetected by neither Danielle, her father, her mother or her best friend Xandria. Nikki had done such great detective work that she was now able to confirm in her own mind that the affair between her father and Danielle actually does exist. The time had finally arrived for her to confront her evil aunt and put an end to this charade.

Nikki thought it best to speak with her Aunt Dannie one on one. She was hoping that her aunt would not come out of the bag on her, but maybe she would be ashamed and not have too much animosity and resentment toward her.

Nikki tried to choose a time that she and Danielle would be alone and free from any interruptions so that they calmly discuss the situation. She had been rehearsing in her mind how she would approach Danielle and what she would say to her. Nikki wanted this confrontation to be over with and done by the time Xandria came to pick her up for their sleep-over.

Today was Thursday and everyone was out about doing their own thing. Her father would be working a little late today because of some special project he was heading and the deadline was fast approaching. Her mother was working the four days on four days off twelve-hour shift at Homestead, so she would be working all night. Danielle was on her way in from a spa/nail treatment and Nikki was at home doing some last minute chores and getting her overnight bag ready for her sleep-over with Xandria.

Now would be a great time to confront Danielle Nikki told herself, as she zipped her overnight bag. She should be home any minute and we can get this affair thing out in the open and over with for good.

Nikki was still up in her room when she hears the front door close. She barely cracks her door open just enough for her to peer through and sees Danielle heading toward her room with some shopping bags in her hands. Nikki decides to allow her a few minutes to get to her room and settle down while she finishes tidying up her room.

Nikki makes her way down the stairs and around the corner to her aunt's room. She swallows hard and takes a deep breath before she softly knocks on Danielle's door.

"Aunt Danielle – may I come in? I'd like to talk to you. It's kind of important," she says nervously.

"Sure Nik – come on in," Danielle chimes.

Nikki slowly opens the door and goes in but senses that this confrontation probably isn't going to be easy for her. She had really started to like her aunt but she detested more what her aunt was doing to her family – especially her mother. The anger that Nikki feels right now toward her father ranks pretty high on Nikki's list of immoral things to do. She feels betrayed by her father almost as much as her mother will probably feel when she has to tell her about the affair between Danielle and her father.

Danielle is sitting on her bed and becks for Nikki to come join her.

"What's on your mind Nikki? You do look a bit serious."

"This is very hard for me to say to you Aunt Danielle but I don't see any other way."

"What in the world are you talking about Nikki – you don't see any other way to do what? Spit it out already. Whatever it is it can't be that hard."

"Well – I know about you and daddy. I know that you all are involved."

"Involved?" Danielle laughs loudly. "What are you saying Nikki? You think me and your father are having an affair? Danielle laughs out loud again. "That's really funny Nikki. That's the best laugh I've had all day."

"I'm not joking about this Aunt Dannie. You and my father are having an affair because I have been watching you all for over a month. I had to be sure."

"Girl you are talking crazy. Now how are you going to sit there and say something like that?"

Danielle tone and body language is changing now and she is starting to become agitated with her niece. She knows that she has been busted but by a little twerp like Nikki.

"Aunt Dannie, you know this is true. There is no use trying to deny it. I have seen you with my own eyes – you and my daddy. For over a month I have watched and followed you two around, but I had to keep you under surveillance long enough that I was sure and that my eyes were not deceiving me."

Now Danielle appeared surprised and didn't know what to say to Nikki at this point. She had under-estimated her niece and had learned that the girl was not the naïve little idiot she thought her to be. She was busted and realized that Nikki would probably go to her mother with this information. Danielle was not prepared for affair to Grant to be made public yet and she couldn't afford to allow her niece to foil her revenge plans.

"Look Nikki – you don't understand. Your father and I go way back – even before you were born. We had a thing before he and your mother married. I could have married him but I stepped aside and allowed him a chance with your mother because I was ready for marriage and had no desire to be tied down. I tried to forget about him afterward but I just couldn't do it Nikki. When I came here, the memories got the better of me and my feelings overcame me. I didn't set out to cause problems for your family," Danielle explains.

"That's not good enough Aunt Dannie and I'm really having trouble believing anything you say right now. You deceived my mom and I honestly feel that you came here for that purpose. How could you do that to her after she lovingly invited you into her home? She loves you Aunt Dannie – why? How could you be so awful to her? The one thing my mom wanted over the years was for you to be back in her life – to be a real sister to her. My mother does not deserve this, especially from you. As much as I know that this will hurt her. I have to tell her the truth about everything."

Danielle had become angry at this point because she realizes Nikki is going to tell her mother everything and she didn't plan all of this and come this far to allow her boneheaded niece to spoil it all and destroy her plans. She was determined to do her revenge on her own terms and would not except anything less.

Nikki gets up off the bed and heads for the door with Danielle right on her heels. When Nikki exits the door, Danielle grabs her firmly by the arm and jerks her back.

"Look – Nikki – you can't do this. Think of what it will do to your mother. This could destroy her and you will be responsible for that," Danielle pleads.

Nikki snatches her arm from Danielle's grip and angrily faces off with her.

"I won't be the one responsible for hurting my mother – you are. My mother doesn't deserve having someone like you for a sister and you're definitely not an aunt of mine," Nikki spouts back with anger. "Now you stay out of my way."

Nikki runs down the hallway and up the stairs toward her room with Danielle chasing after her. Danielle catches up to her at the top of the stairs and grabs her by the arm again and is enraged with fury.

"Nikki – I'm telling you – I can't let you do this. You will NOT spoil my plans. You are as pathetic as your bitch ass mother. I hate Melina – I always have. Now I finally have my revenge. I slept with Grant and now I'm going to have his baby. How do you like that?"

Danielle laughs sarcastically and looks at Nikki as if her eyes could shoot daggers.

"And you – you sanctimonious little bitch can't do anything to stop me. You are no match for me little girl because you are out of your league," Danielle yells.

Tears were flowing freely down Nikki's angelic face. The words of her aunt cut through her soul. The hateful, venomous, and hurtful words were verbal abuse and Danielle knew how to verbally abuse. Children are vulnerable and believe most everything they hear, even teenagers. Though Nikki was wise beyond her years, the sting of Danielle's words hurt to the very core of her being.

Nikki pulls away from Danielle and reaches for the door knob to enter her bedroom.

"You get back here you little bitch," Danielle yells, jerking Nikki back toward her. "You can't just walk away from me."

"My mother will know what kind of evil person you are," Nikki cried.

Danielle had to stop Nikki from exposing he and her plans. She simply couldn't let her tell her mother about any of this because she wouldn't be able to hurt her sister the way that she wants. She wouldn't have the satisfaction of gloating about what she had done to Melina. Therefore, Danielle needed to stop Nikki from spilling the beans. Her niece was causing her too much grief and a lot of anger.

Nikki was trying to pull away from Danielle again, struggling to make it to her room. This time Danielle was fed up with her niece's attempts to get away from her.

"I told you to get back here," Danielle yelled angrily.

Danielle grabs Nikki by both arms, spins her around, and shoves her backwards down the stairs. She stands there at the top of the stairs watching as her niece rolls, flips, and bounces off the stairs until she reaches the bottom and lay motionless on the floor.

"I told you not to mess with me little girl but you wouldn't listen," Danielle shouts.

Danielle slowly walks down the stairs until she reaches Nikki. She stands over her smiling contently as if she were proud of what she had just done.

"See – I told you – I warned you. You know – you brought this upon yourself. You are such a stupid little bitch. Look at you now. You can't do a damn thing to me."

Danielle walks away nonchalantly and goes back to her room, retrieves her purse, and leaves the house not giving even a second thought to Nikki who is still lying on the floor unconscious.

About a half hour later, Xandria arrives at the house to pick up her friend Nikki. She knocks on the door but gets no answer. She also calls, but her calls are unanswered and go straight to voicemail. Xandria decides to try peeking through a crack in the curtain to see if she could see anything in the house. She's almost floored when she spots her friend lying on the floor and not moving.

"Oh my god – Nikki!" she cries.

Xandria quickly dials 911 and requests an ambulance. The next call she places is to Nikki mom. She tells her that Nikki is hurt and appears to have fallen down the stairs and to meet her at Saint Elizabeth Regional Medical Center. Melina began crying profusely but she manages to calm down enough to explain to her co-workers that she had to leave. Melina calls Grant before she leaves Homestead and informs him about Nikki's accident and which hospital to go to.

On the way to Saint Elizabeth all of Melina's thoughts were on Nikki and hoping that she was not hurt badly. She prayed like never before and hoped that her daughter would be okay.

Chapter

Fourteen

Nikki's mom and her friend Xandria were at the hospital with her and Grant had just arrived. He was distraught with worry and concern.

"I just don't understand how something like this could have happened. I heard that it was a while before Nikki was found. How long was it before she got help?" Grant asked angrily.

"I think about an hour Mr. Harrington because I had last spoken to her around four o'clock. I arrived at the house and found her a little after five," Xandria said humbly.

"My God –- my poor sweet baby girl. She has got to pull through this. She just has to."

A doctor entered the room and identified himself as Dr. Khumalo. He said that Nikki was stable but, she had blunt force trauma to her head and a broken arm and that he had concerns about the head injury. Dr. Khumalo told them that Nikki had never regained consciousness and that the MRI indicated very little brain activity.

Dr. Khumalo had delivered devastating news to Nikki's family. Nikki was unresponsive, with fixed and dilated pupils, and had quickly diagnosed a traumatic brain injury. Only a ventilator was keeping her alive. A subsequent fall down a flight of stairs had changed the course of Nikki's life and that of her family. Dr. Khumalo had given Nikki's condition a name --- TBI. TBI is an acquired brain injury that disrupts the normal function of brain with varying degree of recovery. TBI results in different abnormal states of consciousness, depending upon the area involved, extent & severity of the injury. In Nikki's case, she was in a coma. A coma is a state of abnormal consciousness where a person is unconscious & unaware, not responding to any external stimuli with no sleep-wake cycle. It is supposed to be the result of diffuse trauma that includes almost all centers of the brain. This state could last for a few days, a few weeks, a few months or to even years, and then may either be reversed to gain consciousness or the patient could enter into a vegetative state or death.

Dr. Khumalo tried to prepare Nikki's family for what they were going to be faced with in regard to her recovery. He had a private conference with them to try to answer any questions that they might have. Nikki's family would ask the question -- WHEN WILL SHE WAKE UP?

Dr. Khumalo would tell them that no one can tell you when she will wake up. You can only WAIT and SEE. Furthermore, head injured persons rarely wake up all at once. Rather the process of full recovery of consciousness is gradual and takes hours in the mildest cases, and may take months or even years in the worst cases, and may take months or even years in the worst cases. Some people improve only to a point and never fully regain awareness of their surroundings.

Nikki's family would ask the question -- IS RECOVERY FROM A HEAD INJURY POSSIBLE?

Dr. Khumalo would tell them -- Yes, in contrast to the short time it takes to injure the brain, recovery is measured in weeks, months and even years. Recovery is most rapid shortly after the injury and slows down with the passage of time. Many people with severe head injuries end up with almost no noticeable problems, but others require constant care for the rest of their life.

Nikki's family would ask the question -- WHAT WILL BE THE ULTIMATE OUTCOME?

Dr. Khumalo would tell them -- Most people who survive a serious head injury eventually wake up from coma, that is, they begin to open their eyes. In the best cases recovery proceeds from this point to NEARLY COMPLETE RECOVERY. In worst cases there is no recovery beyond opening their eyes. People who wake and sleep but have no meaningful interaction with the world around them are said to be in PERSISTENT VEGETATIVE STATE. This is probably the worst possible outcome. In between these extremes is a very wide range of outcomes, some fortunate, and some tragic. It is very important to know that the outcome may remain UNKNOWN for many months.

Nikki's family would ask the question -- WHEN WILL WE KNOW HOW BAD NIKKI"S HEAD INJURY IS?

Dr. Khumalo would tell them -- It may seem cruel and uncaring when he says we just have to WAIT and SEE but this is the accurate answer. In general terms, the longer a person remains in coma, the less likely he/she is to recover completely. The process of recovery almost always takes much longer than the family and friends expect. A few people may eventually become essentially normal after several months in coma, whereas others may suffer devastating permanent injury after only a brief period of coma. As would be expected, people with head injuries generally do better if just their head is injured and they do not also have serious injuries to other parts of their bodies.

Nikki's family would ask the question -- WILL NIKKI DIE?

Dr. Khumalo would tell them -- No one can accurately predict whether a head injured person will die. Head injuries are often serious enough themselves to cause death. There are two critical periods in the immediate recovery of a head injured person. The first is in the first day or two after the injury when the injuries may be so overwhelming as to cause death in the face of the most intensive treatment. Those who survive this period face another critical period beginning a few days later and continuing for two weeks or more. This critical period results from swelling of the injured brain.

Grant clenched his teeth and shook his head at the information that Dr. Khumalo was telling them. He was in such disbelief that his beautiful daughter was in this state and he was about to lose it.

"So you are telling us that our Nikki is in this coma and you have no idea when or if she will come out of it?" Grant asks angrily.

"You are correct Mr. Harrington – and I am very, very sorry to have to give you this sort of news," Dr. Khumalo states with empathy. "If there is anything that I can do for you all please let me know. Again – I am very sorry."

Melina becomes hysterical and starts wailing uncontrollably. The thought of her daughter being in a coma was nearly unbearable. Thoughts of how she would miss seeing Nikki's beautiful smile and her upbeat personality made her heart hurt even more. Melina also realized that she would have to pull strength from her deep rooted spiritual beliefs and ethics. Now was the time to draw from her spirituality and strong faith in God to see her through this overwhelming time in her life.

Chapter

Fifteen

Several weeks have gone by and Nikki seems to have not improved at all. Nikki's best friend Xandria sits by her bedside sadly watching the ventilator work and breathes for her friend. She is still having trouble believing that Nikki is in this state and doesn't understand how something like this could have happened. Xandria's heart aches for her friend as she remembers happier times they spent together. Xandria thinks back on what Dr. Khumalo had said about coma patients and their possible recovery. He had said that there was no one treatment that can cause someone to come out of a coma, but treatments could prevent further physical and neurological damage, however.

Dr. Khumalo had tried to ensure that the Nikki wasn't in any immediate danger of dying. He was the doctor that had placed the tube in the Nikki's windpipe through her mouth, and hooking her up to a breathing machine, or ventilator. If there had been any other serious or life-threatening injuries to the rest of her body he dealt with them in the order of decreasing severity. He felt that the excess pressure in her brain caused the coma, and for a short time had surgically placed a tube inside her skull to drain the excess fluid. A procedure called hyperventilation, which increases the rate of breathing to constrict blood vessels in the brain helped to relieve pressure too. The doctor has Nikki on medication to prevent seizures. At one point Dr. Khumalo thought that Nikki may have acute ischemic strokes and had said that she would have to undergo procedures or receive special clot-busting medication in an effort to restore blood flow to the brain if that happened.

Doctors used imaging studies often, such as magnetic resonance imaging (MRI), or computed tomography (CT) scans, to look inside Nikki's brain and identify pressure and any signs of damage to the brain tissue. Electroencephalography (EEG) was a test that was used to detect any abnormalities in the brain's electrical activity. This test could also show brain tumors, infections, and other conditions that might have caused the coma. The doctor had also suspected meningitis, and had performed a spinal tap to make the diagnosis by inserting a needle into the Nikki's spine and removing samples of cerebrospinal fluid for testing.

After all of these tests were done and Nikki was stable, the doctors concentrated on keeping her as healthy as possible. Coma patients are susceptible to pneumonia and other infections. Many comatose patients stay in the hospital's intensive care unit (ICU), where doctors and nurses can continually monitor them and this was where Nikki was kept. People who are in a coma for a long time may receive physical therapy to prevent long-term muscle damage. Nurses moved Nikki periodically to prevent bedsores -- painful skin wounds caused by lying in one position for too long.

Because patients who are in a coma can't eat or drink on their own, they receive nutrients and liquids through a vein or feeding tube so that they don't starve or dehydrate. In addition to her feeding tube, Nikki was receiving electrolytes -- salt and other substances that help regulate her body processes.

Dr. Khumalo had warned that if Nikki continued to be dependent on a ventilator to breathe, they may need to place a special tube that goes directly into her windpipe through the front of the throat called a tracheotomy. The tracheotomy tube can be left in place for extended periods of time because it requires less maintenance and does not injure the soft tissues of the oral cavity and upper throat. Because was in a coma couldn't urinate on her own, they placed a rubber tube called a catheter inserted directly into her bladder to remove the urine.

Xandria quietly cried for Nikki and couldn't face the possibility that she may not experience the closeness that she and her friend had once shared as best friends.

Melina walks up and gently places her arms around Xandria. She cradles her head in her bosom as she would have done for her own child.

"You know Xandria - Nikki is a very strong young woman. She will eventually beat this and come back to us. We just have to believe it sweetie".

Xandria's arms encircles Melina's waist as they hold each other up in quiet strength. Both are looking forward to the day that Nikki will open her eyes again.

Grant suddenly has a revelation and asks – "Has anyone let Danielle know about what's happened to Nikki?"

"No – I didn't think about it," Melina replied.

"Well, I will call her and let her know," Grant said.

Grant tried calling Danielle's phone, but it ringed until it went to voicemail.

He tried calling her phone again and still no one answered.

"Melina – – I can't seem to get her so I'm going to see if I can locate her,"

Grant said on his way out the door.

"Mrs. Harrington – I appreciated your support earlier and if I can do anything for you would you let me know?" Xandria asks innocently.

"Sure sweetheart – and thanks for getting Nikki here."

"No worries Mrs. Harrington. Nikki is my friend and I love her like a sister."

Xandria softly smiles, walks over to Melina and hugs her.

"You know what Mrs. Harrington? You're like a second mother to me and I will be here for you as you have for me. I believe now that Nikki will be back with us. You know that I love her like a sister."

"I know baby – I know. You go a hate and take care of your business. If there are any changes I will let you know."

"Okay Mrs. Harrington. I'll see you soon."

After Xandria leaves, Melina turns her attention back to her daughter. Though she was having trouble understanding how something like this happened, she still remains hopeful that Nikki will make a full recovery. She gently gathers her daughter's hand in hers and holds it to her face.

"My sweet, sweet angel girl – you have to come back. You are so bright, full of life, and have your whole life ahead of you. I am so happy you are my daughter – my precious little flower who is always in bloom. I watch and admire you as each and every milestone looms around the corner. It seems like it was only yesterday that we shared a breath, but now it seems like tomorrow you could leave and I would be left alone. You started as my tiny little angel who was much like a beautiful jeweled hummingbird that's always in flight. When you came into my life you brought me so much joy. You are such a beautiful young lady and I am so proud to be your mommy. The perfect little princess is what you are and I thank the Lord above for you each and every night. How did I get so blessed to have as sweet of a gift as you. You are the love of my life – I will always help you ---- and I will always be here for you my precious beautiful Nikki.

Grant has been all over town looking for Danielle to tell her about what happened to Nikki. He finally locates her at one of several hotels they have shared. After knocking on the door, Danielle lets him and immediately notices that something is off kilter with him.

"What's wrong Grant?" Danielle asks in a non-chalant manner.

"It's Nikki --- she is in a coma after falling down the stairs," Grant shares.

"Oh really ---- she fell down some stairs uh?"

"Why are you acting like that Danielle. I thought you'd liked Nikki. You act like you could care less about what has happened to my daughter."

"Honestly Grant ---- I don't care. I tried to tell you the little gal that she was out of her league dealing with me but she wouldn't listen. I don't appreciate people getting into my business. Plus she kept threatening to tell her stupid ass mother about us. You know that I wasn't going to let her mess up my plans."

Grant had begun to have a realization about what had happened to his daughter after listening to all of the things Danielle had just said. He was secretly hoping that he wouldn't have the heart to hurt a child. The mere thought of Danielle possibly doing bodily harm to his daughter was unthinkable. As crazy as he knew he was -- even Danielle wouldn't do something that despicable.

"Danielle – look. I am dead serious here and I need for you to answer this question for me. Did you have anything to do with Nikki's fall?"

"You damn right I had something to do with her fall. Hell I shoved the little bitch down the stairs. I told her to stay out of my business and not go to her mother with these accusations. But no-o-o-o-o-o ---- she couldn't do that. That's why after she had fallen, I walked past her and told her that's what she gets for fucking with me," Danielle viciously spouts.

Grant could not believe what he was hearing coming out of Danielle's mouth. Not only had she helped him to destroy his marriage to Melina but she brazenly to putting his daughter in this comatose condition.

Struggling to contain his extreme anger, Grant rushes Danielle and begins choking her. At this point he didn't care anymore because he had lost everything he held dear ---- is wife who he loves dearly and now his precious daughter Nikki. He didn't know if she would ever regain consciousness.

Danielle was trying to pull Grant's hands from her neck, but her efforts were futile. All she managed to get out was that she had called security before he got there. Danielle knew Grant would lose it when he learned of her involvement in Nikki's fall.

Grant refused to refrain from choking Danielle even though he knows security is on the way. It is so delirious with anger that he doesn't realize he is getting close to strangling Danielle. She collapses to the floor still fighting with him, clawing at his hands clasped around her delicate neck, but it is to no avail. Danielle refused to give up and continued fighting for her life, scratching at Grant's hands and drawing blood. His grip only tightened around her neck and she could feel her life slipping away as her hands began getting limp and gradually began falling to the floor.

Danielle's eyes had become watery and red and the veils in her face were becoming enlarged. She is sensing the life draining from her quickly weakening body as she starts to succumb to death's grip. As her eyes began closing she could feel Grant's grip loosening from around her neck.

Security had finally arrives and pulls Grant off of Danielle, but they had to work extremely hard to get him restrained and handcuffed. Danielle was gasping for air over and over again. When Danielle finally was able to speak, she a screeched, "I want that son of a bitch arrested. He tried to kill me and I am pregnant."

Danielle was actually about four months pregnant, but you couldn't tell it. Her breasts had enlarged but that wasn't much of a baby bump which had helped to cloak her pregnancy.

Grant, still seething with anger from Danielle admission of her involvement in his daughter's near fatal fall didn't believe a word of this shit about her being pregnant.

"You crazy bitch -- you are not carrying my child."

Security had called on the LPD (Lincoln Police Department) and two of their officers had just arrived. The police were called after security managed to get Grant restrained.

"This woman here openly admitted to me that she pushed my daughter down the stairs. I want her arrested," Granted raved.

"Look -- Mr. Harrington. I'm officer Perelli and I know nothing of this incident you are referring to. But a call was made to us about you strangling this woman.

Security actually witnessed you strangling her. So I have no choice sir but to place you under arrest."

Danielle walked over to the bed and plopped down. She had the most content look on her face. For her, Grant's arrest would assure her being able to accomplish her goal of destroying her sister's life.

The officer began reading Grant his rights aloud. "You have the right to remain silent, anything you say can and will be used against you in a court of law, you have the right to have an attorney present during questioning, if you cannot afford an attorney, one will be appointed to you free of charge. Do you understand these rights as I have explained them to you sir?"

Grant stood there with his a dropped in dismay. He could not believe that he was being charged and that it could be very serious thanks to Danielle setting him up the way that she did.

"Yes officer -- I understand my rights," Grant reluctantly replied.

"I need you to come with us now," Officer Perelli said.

Grant quietly exits the room with the two officers leaving Danielle to gloat in her success.

Chapter

Sixteen

Melina soon discovers she has more bad news to face when she learns of Grant's arrest. She didn't want to leave her daughter's side but had to see if she could get her husband out of jail and find out what happened. At this point, she is feeling like her world is being picked a part by some unknown entity. With so much chaos going on in her life right now, Melina's strong faith will be tested.

After arriving at the police station Melina searches for someone to ask about Grant. She really didn't know what to expect but she did know that bailing someone out of jail could be potentially expensive depending on the charges.

Momentarily, and officer enters the room and approaches Melina.

"Ma'am -- may I help you?"

Melina smiles weakly at the officer. She is nervous and unsure about how to get Grant released.

"Yes…uh…I…I… want to try to get my husband out of jail. He told me he had been locked up here but I am not sure how to go about this bail process. Oh … officer… I am sorry… the name is Melina Harrington. I apologize for not introducing myself."

"Well that's quite all right Mrs. Harrington. I am Officer Mark Taylor. And as I was saying Mr. Harrington has been charged with attempted murder."

"What? Attempted murder?"

"Please… calm down Mrs. Harrington, okay?"

"I am so sorry for that outburst Officer Taylor, but that charge was a bit of a shock for me. But there must be some mistake. Grant wouldn't try to kill anyone."

"Mrs. Harrington, hotel security walked in on him still strangling this woman. Security was the ones who reported at him. They literally had to pull him off of the lady."

"That just doesn't sound like Grant. He has never had any demented tendencies such as trying to kill somebody. We have had some serious disagreements before and he has never raised his hand to me. This is why I'm having so much trouble believing that he tried to kill someone."

"All I can tell you is that Mr. Harrington is charged with felony assault by strangulation."

"Who is this woman he supposedly tried to kill?"

The officer pauses and looks at the paperwork.

"According to this paperwork the lady's name is Danielle Jackson," Officer Taylor replied.

"Danielle Jackson? Now I know there has to be a mistake. Danielle is my sister. This can't be right… it just can't be."

"This is the name listed on the paperwork."

"Well I'm going to have to get to the bottom of this. Why would Grant try to kill Danielle? This makes no sense. He was only going to let her know what had happened to Nikki. Officer Taylor… where do I need to go to get release papers started so that I can get my husband out of here?"

"Go to booking and ask the booking officer whether or not it is a cash bond only situation. In the case of a cash bond, you cannot go through a bail bondsman. Next, ask for the amount of the cash bond and when can you pick him up. Arrive at the jail with cash in hand. Pay the booking officer the full amount of the cash bond. When Mr. Harrington is formally released, he will be released into your care."

"Thanks for explaining that procedure to me. I do appreciate that. Do you think that I could see Grant for a moment?"

"Sure Mrs. Harrington. I'll take you back."

Melina followed the officer down a long corridor and through some double doors. They walked past several cells before arriving at the one where Grant was being held.

"I'll give you all some privacy. Just let me know when you are done, okay?"

Melina nodded her head in agreement and smiled dimly at the officer as he exited the door.

After the police officer had gone, Melina turns her attention to Grant. Eyeing her husband she tries to understand how her husband of nearly 20 years could be locked up for strangulation/attempted murder… and it is the strangulation/attempted murder of her own sister no less. What could have been so bad that it caused Grant to become angry enough to try to kill my sister she thought?

Grant still cannot make eye contact with Melina. He realizes that he has totally ruined their marriage and felt that his wife wouldn't be able to get past such huge indiscretions. He'd had an on-going affair with his sister-in-law and then he had gotten her pregnant. At any rate, he had pretty much accepted the fact that his marriage to Melina was over and that it was just a matter of time before she learned everything.

Melina clears her throat and swallows hard, preparing herself to speak. She didn't know what kind of answers Grant would give her to her questions but his answers needed to be some damn good ones.

"Grant – you want to explain what's going on here? The police officer said you were strangling Danielle and that they had to drag you off of her."

Grant walks over to the cot and slowly sits down. He still wouldn't look at Melina and now he wouldn't answer her. He just sat there displaying that *"I have lost everything near and dear to me"* look.

Grant's silence was agitating Melina. Hearing her and deliberately refusing to answer was only making things worse between him and Melina. Then there was the fact that their daughter was in a coma in which no one really knew if she would wake from looming over their heads. With so many things to contend with, Melina was overwhelmed and could not withstand anymore disappointments or misfortunes.

"Grant --- do you wish to answer me because I know you hear me. I don't have the patience for this. You need to answer me ---- now. I can't handle your bullshit right now. Tell me why you were strangling my sister. I want some answers and I'm trying to help you get out of here. You're charged with felony assault by strangulation and maybe even attempted murder --- do you understand? This is a serious charge and you could get serious jail time for this if you're convicted."

Melina's words appear to be falling on deaf ears as Grant only continues being silent --- just sitting there on the cot with his head hung down.

Melina clenches her teeth, shoots Grant an evil eye and then shakes her head. She thinks to herself, *this stubborn ass man is really trying my patience. Now he's just going to sit there like a knot on a log and act like he doesn't hear me. I almost feel like walking over to him and slapping the hell out of him. Maybe he will respond to that. The man sitting in front of her now is acting like someone she doesn't even know. He's acting totally out of character and won't even respond to me. Who the hell is this man? Why won't he say something --- just anything in his own defense? The man before me now used be larger than life but now sits here just a shadow of his former self ---- looking regretful, worthless, and grief-stricken. I just don't understand nor do I know what to make of his appearance or his actions right now.*

"Grant --- I've got to get back to Nikki. I can't stay here all day trying to extract information from you. Our daughter needs me. So if you want me to help you, please say something ---- anything."

Grant finally makes a motion to respond to Melina after sitting there with an expressionless stare for such a prolonged period of time. He slowly raises his head and looks Melina square in the eyes.

"You take care of our daughter. Don't worry about me. I brought this upon myself and will just have to deal with the consequences," Grant states.

Grant swallows hard and pauses momentarily, repositioning himself on the cot. And then continues.

then disappears. Melina was at a lost and her over-worked, tired mind and body was starting to shut down on her. The one thing that she did know was that she needed to try to get some rest so that she could be there for Nikki.

Chapter

Seventeen

Today started out as a beautiful day. Melina had gotten up, showered, dressed, and had eaten her usual bagel with strawberry cream cheese. She was sitting on her window seat at the bay window slowly enjoying her cup of coffee. Officer Taylor had called her shortly after she'd made coffee and fixed her bagel. He informed her that Grant's hearing was going to be around 10am that morning. As she looked out of the window to the park in the distance her mind drifted back to her conversation with Grant. The entire conversation had been weird and had left her with many unanswered questions. One lingering question haunted her. What could Danielle have done that would have caused Grant to strangle her she asked herself? Then there was the other question which was why would Grant say that I would hear bad things being said about him. After thinking about all these things for a while Melina came to the realization that since Grant had been that angry with Danielle it had to be something severe. Furthermore, Grant would not have had any reason to come so close to killing my sister unless it was a serious situation.

Melina was in such deep thought that she never heard Danielle enter the room.

"Good morning Lina," Danielle said in a raised tone breaching Melina's thoughts.

"How is Nikki doing?"

"There's no change. She is still comatose," Melina said displaying a saddened expression on her face.

"I am so sorry Lina. I know this has to be hard on you. If there is anything I can do to help you, please let me know. I just want to be there for you."

Melina turns to Danielle and faces her with a solemn look on her face.

"There is something you can do Danielle."

"Sure Sis --- what is it? Just name it."

"You can tell me what happened between Grant and you. What could have made him angry enough to strangle you?"

Danielle closely searches Melina's face for signs of her being naïve. As soon as she spotted a hint of her being unsuspecting, Danielle pounced on it with both feet.

"I was trying to tell Grant that you could use a brand new living room suite and you were worth spending any amount of money on. He said that there was nothing wrong with the furniture that you all have. You know me sis --- I get flip sometimes and I called him a cheap mother fucker. Grant lost it and before I knew it he had his hands around my neck choking the hell out of me."

"The police officer stated that there were two witnesses -- I believe he said security or something," Melina said.

"Yeah, I rode with Grant to Kohl's department store and this was where the altercation took place. If it had not been for security, I hate to think what might have happened to me. I was really scared and had never seen Grant angry like that before."

Well Danielle, at least now you know you can't say things like that too Grant."

"Guess not," Danielle replied.

"Do you want to ride with me to the hospital to be with Nikki?" Melina asks.

"No sis -- I'm sorry. I have an appointment but you know I will have my niece in my prayers."

"Oh – okay -- I'll see you later?" Melina says.

"Of course Lina," Danielle says on her way out of the door.

Melina contemplates Danielle's answers to her questions momentarily and decides that things could have happened just as she said. But in the back of her mind Melina still didn't see why Grant would that angry about being called out of his name. She was sure that her husband has probably been called worse. Maybe he just had an off day.

Grant's bail hearing was also today. To be released he had to persuade the judge that he is not a danger to the community and that he was not a flight risk. He had acquired his own lawyer to plead his case and had supplied the lawyer with proof that he isn't likely to run.

Melina had eased into the hearing unnoticed by Grant. She wanted to listen in on the proceedings. She sat quietly in the back of the room near the door so that she could leave undetected too.

Grant had called Melina once to ask if she would bring him a change of clothes. She did of course because she wanted to help her husband and he also loved him. Melina sat quietly in the back of the courtroom and watched as her husband and his lawyer talked.

Melina's mind drifted momentarily back to the time when she and Grant had first met. He was a simple, honest, sophisticated young man with high morals. He was tall, athletic, handsome, intelligent, and very considerate. Grant swept Melina off her feet and had won her heart all those years ago. Looking at Grant now, Melina still sees that handsome, tall, athletic, intelligent man but with the addition of a slight hit of gray mixed in here and there. In Melina's eyes, his highlights of gray only added to his sophistication.

Grant listened attentively as his lawyer explained things to him. His lawyer advised him not to speak unless directed to do so by him. The lawyer asked Grant about his ties to the community and about any negative factors. Although he would be speaking, Grant was informed that the judge would be looking carefully at him trying to tell if he was reliable. Therefore Grant's facial expression and body language count for a great deal. The lawyer had told Grant not look angry, even if he had been wrongfully arrested, not to allow his gaze to wander, and to keep his attention focused on the judge. The lawyer had asked that he not cross his arms over his chest as it would portray the appearance of being challenging, that he needed to stand up straight and behave with respect and dignity. The only issue being decided today is whether to let Grant out of jail while awaiting his trial.

Grant obeyed his lawyer's advice and maintained a respectful appearance to the judge and was rewarded for it. After consideration of the documents furnished to him by Grant's lawyer, the judge allowed Grant to be released until his trial.

After hearing the judge's ruling, Melina quietly exited the courtroom and returned to her daughter's side at the hospital. There had still been no change in her condition, and to Melina she just appeared to be asleep. But she held Nikki's hand each day and talked to her about all of the everyday things that happened at home.

Melina was told that even though Nikki has suffered severe head trauma, her hearing could very well be stable and she possibly could be aware of everything that is said, but just not be able to respond. So Melina would hold conversations with Nikki about old times. She thought that it would be great to hear encouraging words from a family member. She believed that just the sound of a family member's voice could be soothing and reassuring. Melina would talk to Nikki and touch her. She didn't know whether not her daughter could feel her touch, but then again she might. Melina knew what a loving touch meant to her so she could only imagine what it would mean to Nikki who could be cognizant of her surroundings.

Melina tried to make sure that she was at the hospital when the doctors made their rounds so that the doctors could keep her abreast of any medical changes in Nikki. The doctors all encouraged Melina to remain hopeful because she played an important role in the possible recovery of her daughter. Should she be blessed and Nikki awakens, she would be surprised of how much her daughter heard and felt and how special her conversations had been to both of them.

Chapter

Eighteen

Nearly two months had gone by and Melina had been diligent in staying with and talking to Nikki daily. Somehow she managed to remain optimistic in light of all the other overwhelming events that have taken place in her life. Melina had taken family sick leave from her job in order to assist with her daughter's care. Although it required round-the-clock work, Melina never considered her daughter's care as a burden and referred to it as being an honor. She loved her daughter so and by all accounts, no one could have done a better job at taking care of her than her own mother.

Each and every day Melina faithfully observed her daughter Nikki being fed through a tube and helped the attending nurse empty urine bags, change diaper pads, and bathe and turn her. She was so dedicated and diligent with the hygiene of her daughter that she never even got a bed sore.

Melina read to Nikki, combed her hair, and rubbed popsicles on her lips… and she never gave up hope that one day she would awaken. She felt deep down that her daughter was strong and would fight her way back to her.

Although Nikki's medical bills were insurmountable, Melina kept her strong faith in God. She knew that she had to be a mother and guardian of a precious soul and didn't take this responsibility lightly.

* * * * *

Today Melina was in a very gratified mood. When she had finished bathing Nikki, the experience had thrust her back into a time when Nikki first made herself known to her. Melina reached back and pulled her chair up close to her bed, placed Nikki's hand in hers, laced their fingers together and lovingly placed the back of her hand to her cheek. A stray tear coursed down her face as she gently rubbed Nikki's hand on her cheek. She laid her weary head close to Nikki's body, closed her eyes, and allowed her subconscious to whisk her mind away to a time when she first became aware of Nikki's first existence.

It was 17 years earlier and I was reclining comfortably on an examination room table that a technician jellied my belly with sonogram goo. Within a few seconds I heard a sound I would never forget for the rest of my life. It was Nikki's rapid, sparrow-small heartbeat. Even though her heartbeat was strangely distorted in its muffled amplification, all I heard was life – precious vital life. There was life inside me – a heart beating inside my womb. It was so hard to believe a human being's heart could beat that fast but then again; Nikki's was no bigger than a hummingbird's at the time. Yet there she was, alive, inside my body, making her presence known. She was undeniable. When I first heard this manic, throttling little drum, she immediately and instinctively understood the power it would forever have over me, and I knew also that Nikki would look to me for her source of survival. Accepting this grand responsibility had come as natural to me as breathing and before Nikki was even born, I had already fallen deeply, unshakably in love with her.

I recognized the racing heart as the sound of love itself. And at that moment, she knew that she would be her one true love – her little valentine girl. Months later, as I had screamed and screeched her into the world, all of the blinding pain that accompanied Nikki's birth was silenced the moment she saw her little angelic face.

Something dramatic was going on "out there" in that hospital room – a big fuss was being made with heart monitors, forceps, and doctors. There was craziness and faces covered by blue masks, but Nikki and I were in our own little world. Nobody could touch us – nobody could enter. Something intensely awesome had just occurred – something miraculous. Still, amiss the hysteria, Nikki and I experienced a frozen moment in suspended animation. I touched Nikki, she felt my touch and we both knew that all of the drama of the world would forever melt away in the bliss of this true love. My valentine was born – my forever girl.

I held her so tightly – and didn't loosen my grip for years. I walked with little Nikki strapped to my body and dangling like a goofball in that baby bjorn baby carrier, my back aching, my nose eternally sniffing the top of her sweet head. I would know that smell blindfolded, even today.

As I watched Nikki grow, my heart expanded with each new step she took. And every time she fell, I felt the pain in ways that only a mother could understand.

Then, of course, there was that awful day that the doctor had misdiagnosed Nikki with leukemia. They told me that Nikki was going to die if she didn't get immediate treatment, and all I could think of was, "No! No! No! – Not my baby – not my sweet little girl! My baby cannot be that sick! She's only seven years old!"

I had ridden in the ambulance with Nikki all the way from Lincoln to Omaha's Children's Hospital and Medical

Center that horrible night. I held Nikki's hand as the tubes went in and out of her frail, little body. Nikki endured test after test and I sat there hiding the reservoir of tears behind my nervous fingers.

But my Nikki was strong.

When the nurses brought Nikki a selection of toys to keep her occupied, she smiled at me and said, "Wow Momma. I thought this was the worst day of my life, but now it's the best day ever."

One silly little toy was all it took to change Nikki's outlook. I almost crumbled in the face of my little daughter's courage.

As it turned out, I learned that Nikki didn't have leukemia at all, but an acute case of ITP, a blood disorder that occurs when the body is not producing enough platelets. This diagnosis was serious, for sure, but not leukemia serious.

Still, I thought -- my poor little girl. But it seemed like there was nothing Nikki couldn't conquer. She moved on, like the radiant pulse of energy and love that she was proving to be and learned to read, write, act, and dance. She would think deep thoughts, grooved on music, challenged me daily, and surprised me constantly.

My Nikki was always a survivor.

Everyday my heart walked around outside of my body. I missed Nikki when she was at school, yet I was delighted at her independence. And when I picked her up each afternoon, the very second that she would park that twelve year old body in the passenger seat next to me, everything in my life suddenly became better.

Melina's mind drifted back to the present as she lifted up her head, still clasping Nikki's hand in hers. She placed a gentle kiss on her small, feminine hands and then ever so calmly massaged her cheek with it.

My sweet little angel girl… Mama is here and always will be… Just come back to me baby… just come back to me, Melina softly whispered.

A slight smile of contentment warmed Melina's face as she remembered loving actions that she still does to this day. In a soft, tender voice she whispered, *Nikki… you are my only child. You're just a few months away from becoming legally a woman. As long as you are here, I will never pass an opportunity to check on you and care for you. I will sit here and watch you sleep. Your smooth, caramel-colored skin and your wonderfully shaped, full lips radiate regal beauty. Watching your chest steadily rise and fall is all the peace I need for right now. You are the greatest thing that has ever happened to me. Your life has given me something I will never ever want to be without. You're brought love into my life as only a child can… a love that will never fade.*

Nikki had just heard her mom's heartfelt words and it saddened her beyond belief. She struggled within her own body to try and respond to her mother but just couldn't manage to break free of her prison. She wanted so much to let her know that she can hear her. Nikki could only speak in her mind. *Momma… I am here. I love you so very much and I know how much I mean to you and that you love me. You have been here with me all this time and caring for me. If I could were only able to tell you that I am so thankful for all of your love. Your love is what has kept me alive and fighting to get back to you. Please don't give up on me Momma… please… don't give up.*

Chapter

Nineteen

Several months have gradually gone by since Nikki's accident and Danielle has never stopped by the hospital or called to check on how her niece was doing. She has been living her life as though it was golden and not caring about anything or anyone except herself and her unborn baby. Grant had been blackmailed into giving Danielle a lot of money and she also has her own. All she was doing was splurging and living it up as though she was some type of wealthy heiress.

Danielle feels secure in her life right now and in the fact that she will have the opportunity to destroy her sister's life. Her dream of demolishing Melina's life was appearing to become an actuality. The time of reckoning is fast approaching and is so close that she can almost taste her victory. Danielle feels secure that her revenge can't be ruined by Nikki because she is in a coma and Grant is not going to spill the beans and reveal his part in aiding her in executing her plan. Therefore Danielle thoughts were that Melina won't know anything about her little sister's plan until she gets ready for her to know.

Today Danielle is off on another one of her shopping sprees. She is approaching four months of pregnancy and is displaying a slight baby bump. Concealing her pregnancy from Melina is still a fairly easy task for her because her older sister has more important issues on her mind and has not really noticed much about her little sister's appearance.

Danielle is very aware of her pregnancy now because the baby moves a lot. Feeling is truly believing when it comes to being pregnant. Since she can actually sense her child inside her body, it is seeping into her head that she is nurturing another human being within. Pregnancy is a life-changing experience. Danielle seems to have surpassed the nausea stage and her meals are staying down much better; her energy level is high too.

Danielle should feel elated being an expectant mother because there is nothing to compare to this experience. But Danielle becoming pregnant was solely a part of her plan to hurt her sister Melina. If she had been a normal expectant mother, being pregnant should be so amazing for her and to recognize the sensations of the tiny little body flexing in her womb. Danielle is so diluted in her mind about this baby that she is only enjoying the fact that her pregnancy is one of the ways that she can hurt her older sister. Danielle is out shopping and registering for every fancy gizmo and gadget out there for her little bundle of joy. But this new mom-to-be may be in for a rude awakening if she hasn't figured it out yet. She has always been a selfish individual thinking only of herself. Danielle needs to start milking the remainder of her pregnancy because it will be the end of an era --- especially the last few weeks. These last days will represent the last time in her life when her world only revolves around Danielle.

Once you are a mother, nobody takes care of you. Mothers don't get sick days and they don't get much sympathy because they are too busy taking care of everybody else. This is it. This is the end of your time to wallow and whine and expect anyone to give a shit. Motherhood should be a beautiful, joyous time. In Danielle's case, she can't share and enjoy these precious motherly moments with family and friends because she conceived this baby the wrong way --- by sleeping with her sister's husband. There is nothing beautiful, joyous, or wonderful about doing something that immoral. Another bad part of this situation is that Danielle is using this baby as a tool to cause pain and suffering. Hell --- even the baby is a victim of circumstances. Still worst in this entire fiasco, Danielle tried to kill her own niece to prevent her from exposing her devious plan of revenge and hurt her mother.

Nothing will prevent Danielle from carrying out her evil, selfish plans of destroying her sister Melina's life. She has lost the capacity to love and care about anyone other than herself. Danielle has become egocentrically extroverted and other people including her own sister are merely used for audiences and a source of stimulation. She's become a risk taker and is ruled by her own needs and desires and not social principles. Danielle thrives off the need for new, emotionally intense experiences and is willingness to take risks to obtain these experiences.

Many of us encounter people whose reactions are puzzling. They are easily hurt and offended. Even when someone is being generous, or kind to them they might react with anger, revengefulness, defensiveness, suspiciousness or aloofness. These are difficult people to have as friends, relatives, and colleagues. In Danielle's case, her actions could end up being detrimental.

* * * * *

Since Grant's release on bail, his relationship with Melina had changed. He refuses to go into any detail about what led to him into strangling her sister Danielle.

Melina senses that there is more to this story and she doesn't understand but she's becoming resentful of Grant for not being honest with her. This secrecy of his discretions is putting a serious strain on their marriage. Melina withdraws and tries to hide her feelings; she mulls them over until she nearly thinks herself into despair. She worries about her problems; she worries about her family; she worries about her husband, her marriage, and her daughter. Melina's fears begin to turn into depression. She masks her pain, deceiving herself and everyone else, until she almost explodes at the slightest provocation.

As her husband, Grant had made the greatest difference in her life than anyone else. He had learned the few basic needs unique to her nature as a woman. He had helped her and allowed her to grow into the beautiful creature God designed her to be. After all, she was the one he married and wanted to stay with forever.

Melina steeps some tea and finds a quiet spot in her home to reflect on her marriage and Danielle and Grant. She goes to her cozy window seat at the bay window. It has a wonderful view of their garden and it was the perfect nook where she could relax and drink her cup of tea. Melina's mind embarks upon a journey of her heart. As she slowly sips her chamomile tea, her mind travels through a time in her past when she and Grant began their journey as husband and wife. *A woman releases her pent up emotions through talking about her thoughts. This is how she finds solutions. She needs someone she can trust, who will listen when she is willing to share.*

She needs a man with whom she is safe, who will let her expose her soul, and share her innermost self. Melina wanted a husband who would listen to her without criticism, judgment or rejection. Grant had been the man in which she shared this part of her life. Consequently, Melina knew that a marriage would suffer the loss of intimacy and trust if she could not share herself with her husband. A husband with a sympathetic ear is rare, but she had found that in Grant.

In Melina's mind she believed that marriage was like fruit salad. A man and a woman: each with unique shapes, textures, and flavors, are complete by themselves. Although, when they are combined, you get a brand new creation. Though, both keep their own identity.

When a man's wife cries, her husband is suppose to embrace her and want to solve her problems. Once she gets a few intelligible words out through her sniffles, and he hears what is bothering her, he holds his head back; sometimes he is even stupid enough to laugh. He then he says, "Oh, is that all. It's so is simple. This was the kind of husband Grant had been to her.

Grant used to look so dumbfounded when she stopped talking. Melina remembered that she would look at him and say, "Never mind! I'll figure it out myself," as she stormed off slamming the door. Melina thought about now and how she was angry and frustrated as well as depressed.

Grant now acts as though he has no clue why she had not been throwing her arms around him, giving him a passionate kisses, and thanking him for all his wisdom and love. Now Grant acted like many other men who wants to give women a solution after hearing only a few details. Never mind that they heard only some of the facts. These men would act as though they did not need to hear it all. They had the answer whether their wives wanted it or not. Overall, their answers may have been right, even if it was unappreciated.

Melina draws on her faith and belief in God. It is God that helps her to stay grounded when all else has failed. Melina thought of how she and Grant's recent argument added pressure to an already strained relationship. She believes that God designed women to keep their emotions in, and release them as they speak.

In her mind, Melina feels that there are four qualities every woman needs from her husband for her sense of security and completeness. By understanding them, he can make an enormous difference in his marriage; transform his home, changing the atmosphere from disappointment, confusion, and indifference to one of peace and oneness of spirit and purpose. A wife aches for guidance when her husband fails to be the spiritual leader. God did not intend for her to lead the family. If a man fails here, he exposes his wife to worry she was not meant to experience. Her life seems out of control. The resulting fear and helplessness forces her to make decisions she should not make. Then she must accept the consequences and sometimes her husband's blame if she makes a wrong choice.

The next thing a wife needs is reassurance that she is meeting needs in her husband's life no other woman can. This is a fundamental need common to all women. She needs him to convince her she is special to him. God made her to be a helpmate. The needs she is meeting in his life must be relevant. The more valuable they are, the more he should compliment and appreciate her.

She will become discouraged if she thinks he is more concerned with the needs of too many other people than he is with her needs. She wants to be an essential part of his world. If she is not, her world can discourage and close in on her.

She needs him to cherish her and enjoy setting aside time for personal conversation. There is a difference between loving her and cherishing her. Most men love their wives whether they show it or not. Few men cherish them. A man cherishes her when he knows her as a person, protects her, and compliments her to others.

Melina believes that a wife must be an essential part of their husband's world, and that his love for her extends beyond what she does for him. He needs to show her that he loves her for her sake and let her know he longs to be with her. She wants assurance that the qualities in her he fell in love with are still important to him. He needs to repeat expressions of his love to her often.

Melina remembered a particular time that she and Grant were at this restaurant. They had left a restaurant several years ago, and Grant had opened the car door for her. The woman in the booth that was seated next to them saw this through the window and slugged her husband and I had laughed. I was smart enough; however, to realize how fortunate I was that my husband enjoyed showing me off in public.

Melina thought of how she and Grant were always so busy during the day that they would sit up talking late many nights. This was usually the only time they were alone. As a woman, Melina would often have emotions bottled up. Through the years, Grant had been a sounding board. Many times he never said anything. He would usually just say, "Urn-hum, yeah. Right." He would draw her out with well-worded questions that helped her work through harbored doubts and fears.

Melina wondered where her loving, understanding, sympathetic husband has gone. She missed him so very much. Right now while her life is in such turmoil is when she needs him the most. Their marriage is failing and she can't seem to reach him. Both she and his daughter need him.

Chapter

Twenty

For several months now, Melina had noticed a shift in the way that she and her husband Grant interacted with one another. They have been doing this dance around their problems almost daily. At first, she had tried to tell herself that time had made them comfortable and that no one could keep the spark burning red hot after so many years. But, she knew that this was different. Rather than losing the spark, Melina felt that they had lost the general feelings of affection and respect for one another. They were living sort of like roommates. There were fights, to be sure, but more troubling to her was the lack of laughter and the fact that her husband seemed to shut himself down and just go into silent mode, which was an entirely new and recent thing she had never experienced with him.

However, when she mentioned the fact that she felt the marriage was in trouble to Grant, he scoffed at this and told her that she was "expecting too much." He conceded that things had changed, but felt it was due more to where they were in their lives than real problems in the marriage. Still, he wasn't willing to do anything to improve things, nor would he admit to any problems. Melina just did not feel right about ignoring what she sensed and felt between them. She wondered if it were possible to fix their situation without his cooperation.

As time went on, Melina did realize that she and Grant's troubled marriage couldn't be savaged by her alone. It seemed pretty clear to her that there was the possibility that Grant may not likely to come around any time soon. If she waited for him, she might well have waited too long. She was afraid that he might only come around once they were at each other's throats or barely acknowledging each other's presence. By this time, a lot of harm would've been done and saving the marriage might be a lot harder than it needed to be.

It was so frustrating and troubling to Melina to think that his apathy could destroy their marriage, but she knew from experience that she wasn't really going to be able to change his mind. However, she did remind herself that she very much had control over one thing - and that was herself. She could very much control how much time and effort she put into her marriage in the coming, days, weeks, and months. She doubted that changing only one person in a marriage would have a huge impact. But as Melina thought more about her circumstances, she assured herself that not only could it have an impact on the marriage, it could absolutely save herself. Melina felt that maybe once she changed her own attitude and her own actions, then the environment in which the marriage is living is invariably going to change one way or the other. And when this happens, the perceptions and feelings follow suit and then change for the better or worst would be inevitable. Melina knew that some type of change had to happen in order for her to be there for her daughter Nikki.

Melina thought of her parents' marriage and how they seemed to love each other so much. She thought of how they had given her and Danielle the best they could and tried to instill a sense of family and love into them. Her parents had good intentions and genuine feelings in their hearts. They supported their household, worked their jobs, look out for Danielle and me, and others that they cared about.

A slight smile adorned Melina's face as a sweet memory of her and Grant's past life. So were the days where they stared into each other's eyes and share their far away dreams.

Sadness suddenly enveloped Melina as the realization of she and Grant's dreams have started to wane. If this situation that she and Grant were in is the normal course of things, then it comes with a high price. She was afraid that the lack of time and concentrated, repetitive effort that was not being poured into the relationship would eventually manifests itself in a lack of intimacy and a new apathy. As the distance widens between the two of them, she senses more trouble.

Melina had tried to gain control over changing up the circumstances and the environment that was deteriorating she and Grant's marriage. But Grant wasn't trying to put his "all" into fixing their marriage. All she can do is to try to control what she can. She remembered what had brought the two of them together. She knew the things that she and Grant had always vowed to do. She knew the promises that they had made together. She also remembered very well when they were sure that they'd always feel the same way about each other forever.

Melina had to take a hard look at her priorities. In truth, a strong and happy marriage would benefit every area in her life. She decided that whether or not she and Grant mended their relationship, she had to focus on Nikki and to do everything in her power to try to help her.

Chapter

Twenty One

Grant's trial date had finally approached. He and Melina had gotten ready to go and were headed out the door when Grant abruptly stops.

"Melina… wait."

Melina stops and turns to Grant. Looking into his eyes she suddenly became overwhelmed with so much emotion because she had not seen this man in months. These eyes that now held hers were filled with affection and compassion. It was through these were the eyes that she had seen all of the love he'd had for her over the years.

This man standing before her right now appeared to be the man she had loved for so long and adorned.

Grant steps to Melina, lifts her trembling hands into his and squeezes them tightly. Melina could see the pleading in his eyes as a stray tear began coursing down his masculine cheek.

"Melina… I am so sorry for pulling away from you all these months. I know that you love me and that you have tried for months to talk to me. I love you too baby… really I do. All I want is to have our life back the way it used to be before Danielle came into it. I want us to try to work through this and to be a real family again. Can we talk about us when this trial is over? You know… we can get through this Melina… together… okay. Please say that we can talk about this. I don't want to lose you… please… can we talk?"

"We can discuss this later Grant. We will be late for court if we don't leave right now," Melina said in serious tone.

"Okay… okay… But I want us to try to work through this Melina. I love you baby and know that we can do this… together," Grant sincerely pleaded.

"Like I said… we can talk about this later," Melina said sternly. Then she turns and exits the house with Grant trailing behind her.

Danielle had been eavesdropping on Melina and Grant's conversation from upstairs. She had been keeping a low profile ever since Grant nearly strangled the life out of her a few months back. She mostly lived at the Embassy Suites hotel so that she didn't have to face Melina or Grant but stopped by on occasion when they were either asleep or out. Danielle had come in late last night and decided to stay so that she could secretly try to find out what was going on with her sister and brother-in-law. After hearing Melina and Grant's conversation, Danielle was not very happy with the things that were said. She definitely had to keep close tabs on this conversation and see what develops because she was determined not to allow them to reconnect. Danielle clinched her teeth tightly and observed Melina and Grant as they talked. She thought to herself, all of the work she had put into destroying Melina's life would not be for nothing. She would have her revenge at all costs.

Melina and Grant exited the house and arrived at court. She seated herself near the back of the courtroom and Grant joined his attorney at the table near the front of courtroom.

Shortly after the trial had begun, Judge Paul Flynn made an astonishing announcement to the court. *I have been made aware of the extreme circumstances that this defendant has endured over the past months. It is my understanding that the defendant's daughter has been comatose during the entirety of her injury. Any person with compassion can relate to and understand the stressful circumstances of such a heart-wrenching situation that* *involves your children. This type of helplessness can make the best person in the world do things that are out of their character. Also, the defendant has been a positive role model and has been much respected for years in his community. It is for these reasons that I am making my ruling today. Grant Harrington… It is my judgment to sentence you to 365 days of probation, 1600 hours of community service as a "Big Brother" with the Big Brother Big Sister Organization, and a $10,000 fine. You are free to go Mr. Harrington.*

Danielle was seething with anger as she sprang up from her seat.

"You can't do that!" she screamed at the judge. "This man deserves jail time for trying to kill me! Lock him up and throw away the key! What kind of judge are you anyway? You can't just let me walk like that!"

Judge Flynn rose from his seat and banged his gavel loudly. "Order in my courtroom." He pointed his finger at Danielle with a very grim expression on his face. "Young lady… you are out of line and very rude. This is my courtroom and I can do whatever I want and you will not disrespect me. You on the other hand will get to know my fury if you disrespect this court again. I am the kind of judge that will have you held in contempt if you express another outburst such as that in my courtroom again."

Judge Flynn slammed his gavel again, "This court is adjourned."

Grant and his attorneys shook hands on their victory. Melina goes to him and they share a very touching embrace. Danielle is stricken with so much resentment that she can no longer stand to see them and marches out of the courtroom.

After leaving court, Melina and Grant go by the hospital to see Nikki. They find her still unresponsive but as beautiful as ever. They each sat on either side her bed holding and stroking her hand. Nikki was loved so much by her parents and she loved them just as much.

Inside her body Nikki was saying, *Mom and Dad… just hold on. I'm trying to get back to you both. I want Aunt Dannie to pay for tearing apart my family. You all also need to know that she tried to kill me to keep me from telling her plans on hurting both of you. Please don't give up on me because I am fighting my way back to you."*

Seeing Nikki in the hospital so lifeless and unresponsive always made her parents so sad. After Melina and Grant got home from their visit, they succumbed to the sadness and found solace in each other. They embraced with love as they had done months before all of this chaos wreaked havoc in their lives. It had been months since they had been this close but now they each wanted it. When Melina and Grant looked into each other's eyes, all of the love came flooding back like a tidal wave over them. Melina gently kissed Grant on his cheek but he turned his head toward her and they ended up sharing a long, deep, passionate kiss.

After sharing such a powerful kiss, Grant gazed lovingly into Melina's eyes, "I love you so very much and have missed you terribly," he said in a husky tone.

"I love you Grant. Can you love me and hold me like you used to?" Melina whispered.

It was as if no further words were needed between Melina and Grant. He showered her with sweet, feathery kisses before releasing his claim on her. When he extended his hand to Melina, she happily obliged him. They walked hand-in-hand to their bedroom softly closing the door behind them.

Grant stepped up behind her and she could feel his warmth. His breath ruffled her hair as she stood still as long as she could. It had been months since Melina and Grant had made love and for both the emotions were running wildly within them. Their passion had gotten so strong that it felt as though a dam was about to break.

Melina turned to Grant and reached up to run her hand along his strong jaw. She traced his lips with her fingers and then she stood on tiptoe and placed her mouth on his. He deepened the kiss and held her up with a firm hand against her waist.

The next thing they knew Melina and Grant were laying across their bed. Melina's needs had overcome her. Grant's lips moved slowly, sensuously over hers. His kisses were gentle, but her mouth opened beneath his and he skimmed the inner surface with the tip of his tongue.

Slowly, tantalizingly, Grant's tongue moved deeper into the warmth of Melina's mouth. With one hand, he cradled her head, and the other, he opened her blouse, and then ran his hand up her thigh and into her intimacy.

Hunger and white, hot need curled inside Melina. The appetite for lovemaking that she had suppressed woke up with a voracious, consuming thirst. Grant's mouth was hot and wet, and he explored her all over as he removed her clothing. Her whole body was jerking with need as he took off his own clothes.

Melina gasped at the knowledge and certainty that there was nothing wrong with his manhood that night. It stood tall and stately and she whimpered with frustration as he kissed her breasts, but withheld that powerful part of him from her.

"Touch me, Melina," he implored in a raspy voice, and she complied.

Melina closed her hand around his shaft, moving slowly up and down the length of it with unrestrained excitement. He groaned and grunted as she savored the feel of him in her hand. Grant was hot, thick, and arched to meet her when he could take the pleasure no longer. He lifted her hips to meet his thrust and sank deeply into her. She cried out in sweet oblivion and knew nothing except the spiraling sensations that sent her skyrocketing to the stars.

Vaguely, Melina heard Grant shout and quiver before he slumped over her; but she couldn't speak in the aftermath of the explosions that ripped through her.

Melina couldn't talk about the emotions charging through her, and Grant respected her silence as he pulled her in closely to him. They fell asleep in each other's arms as they had done so many times before. Now almost all seemed right in their world as they had begun finding their way back.

Chapter

Twenty Two

Melina and her husband Grant seemed to be getting their faltering marriage back on track. They began doing many of the things that they used to do before their seventeen years of wedded bliss began falling by the wayside. Both have decided that they wanted to fight for the marriage and knew that they would have a long road ahead of them in repairing it. They had learned that the things that people in love did to each other they would remember, and if they were to stay together, it's not because they forget, it's because they learn to forgive. Melina and Grant knew that one of the best things in life is sharing a great experience with someone you love. Activities that had been only ho-hum when done alone could become highly entertaining when done with a partner or spouse. Shared experiences build memories and bond a couple together more closely.

Married couples or other couples who have been together for a long time often get caught up in the cares of daily life. They spend so much time paying bills, taking care of kids, and working that they forget they started out as best friends who had a lot of fun together. Developing a sense of fun is important in keeping a healthy marriage. Melina and Grant used to always make time for each other; and they used to talk and do fun, enjoyable things together.

For the next few months, Melina and Grant started doing things together such as jointly giving time to a good cause such as their mutual love for doing the Big Brother Big Sister volunteering. They began taking some ballroom dance classes at the local community center and they would take turns cooking for each other. Melina and Grant found that hiking and swimming together was entertaining and created memorable experiences that they would be able to look back on many years later. Being active together, whether it's walking, jogging, or playing tennis was keeping the two of them connected in more ways than one. It was also fun to volunteer for a good cause together, whether it's serving soup to the homeless or offering to work as a team with your spouse to spruce up the landscaping at their church building.

Melina and Grant would set aside one night a week to do something fun together and make it a date night. They were a busy couple with hectic schedules and their daughter Nikki relied on their support at the hospital and both visited her regularly. Whatever their schedule, they tried setting a regular date for having fun together and found that it built anticipation and gave them something to look forward to in the middle of a hectic week.

Melina and Grant having fun together made their relationship stronger. It reminded them of why they fell in love with each other in the first place and it was helping to keep the romance alive. It was this "having fun with your mate" lesson was the good example that they wanted their daughter Nikki to see as of how a marriage or partnership should be.

Danielle had been quietly observing Melina and Grant's new found togetherness and was highly enraged by it. She kept her distance from them but stayed on top of the things that her older sister and brother-in-law did. Danielle found it hard to contain her disgust and anger because she did not want the two of them mending the rift in their marriage. Wild emotions swirled around in her head as she thought to herself, *that bitch sister of mine thinks that she is going to fix her marriage to Grant but I will not stand for it. Their little twit of a daughter thought that she could get in my way but I showed her little ass. She should have died when I shoved her ass down the stairs. Lina is still going to pay if it's the last thing I ever do. She will not win this one and I'm going to see to that.*

Danielle was nearing her sixth month of pregnancy now and was being tired a lot. In this second half of her pregnancy she has started setting up her baby's nursery. During her last check-up, she had found out the sex of the baby and was filling up the room with blue décor and clothes. She had decided that now was the time to start sporting her maternity clothes and taking birthing classes for her upcoming birth. Danielle had actually planned for Grant to do birthing classes with her but it was impossible now since her near death experience at his hands.

At this point in her pregnancy, the sixth month, she wanted to make sure that Melina knew that she was expecting but did not yet want her to know the paternity of her baby. Danielle had done well in cloaking her pregnancy from her sister since Melina had been so preoccupied with more pressing issues of her own. They rarely spent much time together which gave Danielle free rein to pursue her plans of destruction of her big sister.

Danielle had to deal with other issues as well in her life other than the downfall of Melina. Her body was going through new changes as her baby was developing within her. Her abdomen had begun to itch due to the stretching of the skin as her baby grew bigger. She had been using body lotion and rubbing it into her skin after baths or when she felt her skin was too dry. Stretch marks had begun populating on her abdomen skin which was stretching to accommodate her baby. Danielle had always taken pride in her looks but keeping her skin moisturized had started becoming a chore. She hated this new symptom in her pregnancy because it was something that she was not able to control. Danielle was quickly realizing that she would not be one of those women to get away with only a few stretch marks… she would not be so lucky. She was experiencing some numbness in her limbs and occasional cramps. However uncomfortable Danielle felt, she was determined to see her plans through to the end to hurt her sister Melina. She was ready to put into action her next phase in her *"destroy Melina campaign."*

Danielle had eavesdropped and heard Grant leave the house so she knew that Melina was alone. It was the perfect time to let her know that she was pregnant. We she came downstairs, Melina was sitting in her favorite spot sipping on a cup of coffee.

"Good morning Lina," she said with a forced smile. "It's a beautiful day out there isn't it?"

"Hello Dannie… yes it is a beautiful day but it would be so much better if my Nikki could see it," Melina sadly replied.

Danielle slowly walked over closer to where Melina was seated looking out unto the park in the distance.

"Uh–h-h Sis… I have some happy news that I want to share with you."

"Well maybe some good news would help get me out of this mood I'm in right now. So… what's the news?" Melina said still watching out of the window.

"I'm pregnant Sis. You're going to be an aunt."

Melina quickly turned her head toward Danielle as she stood there with her hand on her little baby bump she had concealed so well. She was in little shock because she had not noticed any changes in her sister before that might would have given her pregnancy away.

"You are pregnant? How far along are you Dannie?" she asked in a worried tone.

"Yes I am pregnant… about six months Sis. It's going to be a boy," Danielle boasted.

Danielle felt wonderful telling her sister this information because she knew that Melina knew nothing of the means of the baby's conception. In her heart of hearts, she wanted to tell her sister so badly that this was her husband's child but had to force herself to wait a bit longer for this disclosure.

"I think that I was pregnant when I got here Lina but didn't know it at the time."

"Well how long have you known Dannie and why had you not said anything until now?"

""I've known for a few months now but I wanted to surprise you with the news.

Suddenly Melina remembered the incident with Danielle and Grant a few months back and was overcome with emotion.

"O-M-G! I just remembered that Grant could have hurt you and the baby," Melina said crossly.

"It's okay Sis… I'm fine and the baby is fine so you don't have to worry. Both of us are healthy according to my doctor. His heartbeat is very strong and he's been moving around like crazy," Danielle said confidently.

"Who is the father and does he know?" Melina asked.

Danielle smiled contently to herself as she thought about how Grant knew the paternity… that the baby she's carrying is his. She was not ready to tell Melina just yet about who the real father of her baby is.

"The father is my boyfriend back in Atlanta and yes he does know he's the father," Danielle said smirking to herself.

"Oh… okay. I am so happy for you and I'm happy about becoming an aunt. This is some good news."

"Well Sis… I got to go to my doctor's appointment. Are you going to visit Nikki today?"

"Yes I am in about an hour," Melina replied.

"I will send up prayers for Nikki Lina and maybe stop by the hospital later."

"Okay Dannie… thanks for sharing the wonderful news with me."

"Sure… anytime Lina. See you later," Danielle said on her way out the room.

Melina continued to sit at the window after Danielle had gone and stared out into the park. She thought about how Nikki would feel to have a new little cousin in her life. Thoughts of how she would feel about having a new little nephew caused her lips to softly curl. But some unforeseen reason Melina felt as though something life-changing was amiss but she didn't truly know the impact it would have on her. She didn't understand why she could not shake the uneasiness that crept in the inner recesses of her mind. Her heart ached for her daughter and she missed her terribly.

Melina also reflected on her and Grant's relationship. They had gotten to a good place now and were rebuilding their marriage and had discussed renewing their vows. The only thing that was missing from her life was Nikki.

Chapter

Twenty Three

Melina dressed and headed out to the hospital. She had routinely and faithfully gone to the hospital daily to see her daughter Nikki, bathe her, sit and talk with her. She refused to give up and lose hope in her recovery and felt that in some way Nikki could hear her.

After arriving to Nikki's door, Melina said a silent prayer and then entered the room. As she approached her bed, Nikki lay there so peaceful and beautiful. Both her hands were lying at her sides palms up, and her long, dark hair was brushed in a way that it gently caressed her angelic face.

"Good morning Mama," Nikki said in silence. *"I'm going to try my best to make it out this time. You need me and I want to be there for you as you have been here for me all of these months."*

Melina pulled up a chair and seated herself next to her bed, reached over and lifted her small hand into her hers, caressing it to her face. A single tear slowly coursed it way down her cheek, as she watched Nikki's chest rhythmically rise and fall.

"Oh-h-h Mama… please don't cry. I'm right here fighting to get out. I love you so much. If only I could squeeze your hand you will know that I can hear you."

Nikki said a silent prayer and tried with all her might to squeeze her mom's hand. She had been trying so desperately to be free again and regain her conscience so that she could expose her aunt for the attempted murderer she is.

"I have to come back now," Nikki told herself. *"Mama needs me… she needs me now."*

Suddenly a huge surge of energy surged through Nikki and she experienced a feeling she had not felt in a long time. She was aware that she was squeezing her mom's hand. She had finally done it.

Melina suddenly pulled Nikki's hand from her face in sheer disbelief. She had to have imagined her hand being squeezed. She had faithfully sat at her daughter's bed for months and never had this sort of thing happen. To prove to herself that she had not imagined the whole thing, Melina reluctantly asks Nikki a question.

"Nikki... baby... if I really did feel you squeeze my hand, please do it again. Can you squeeze my hand again sweetheart?"

Nikki silently rejoiced, *"I did it... I did it... I finally did it. Now if I can only do it again.*

"Nikki... sweetheart... squeeze mama's hand," Melina recited softly.

This time Nikki didn't have to try as hard to get her hand to move. She silently told her hand to squeeze her mother's hand and she did it.

Melina sprang from her seat still holding unto Nikki's hand. She now looked into her face and could see her daughter's eyes rapidly moving back and forth underneath closed eyelids. Melina observed as Nikki clumsily brings her other hand to her face and tries to pull at the tubes in her nose.

"Come on baby girl... you are nearly there. Just keep going... come on back to me Nikki," she pleaded.

Nikki eyelids were slowly opening and closing as she tried to focus and adjust to the brightness of the lights. Melina quickly pushed the call button and yelled for a doctor to come.

Nikki's eyes were half open and she seemed to be staring into space. Then she slowly turned her head toward Melina, trying to bring into focus the familiar image standing by her bed.

"Mama...?" she said groggily.

"Oh baby... you came back. You did it. I have my baby back," Melina cried.

Dr. Khumalo suddenly entered the room and was amazed to see Nikki lying there with her eyes open. A nurse followed closely behind him holding a chart.

"Mrs. Harrington... I need to check your daughter's reflexes and perform a few preliminary tests."

Nikki... sweetheart... I'm going to step out for a while to let the doctor check you out okay? I'm not going anywhere," Melina said gently.

"Okay mama."

Melina walked out the Nikki's room and went down the hallway to a vacant waiting room. She wanted to call Grant and share the news of their daughter's awakening.

Grant's phone rings several times but on the fourth ring he answered.

"Hello... Grant Harrington here," he spoke in a professional tone.

"Grant... this is Melina. I have wonderful news. Nikki is awake... our daughter is awake," she said, barely able to contain her joy.

"What? Nikki's awake? I'll be right there honey."

After the brief conversation with Grant, Melina continued to sit in the waiting area for a while. Her emotions were running rabid throughout her body causing her entire body to quiver with both excitement and disbelief. This was a day that Melina was not sure would ever come but had prayed so long for over the past months. She was so overwhelmed by the goodness of God giving her daughter back to her and realized how truly blessed she had been. Melina felt the overpowering need to offer up a prayer of gratitude to God. She simply could not this moment to offer up her thankfulness to God for this blessing in her and Grant's lives.

Melina lowered her head in silent prayer as she thought to herself, *Thank you, Lord, for the blessings you have bestowed on my life. You have provided me with more than I could ever have imagined. You have surrounded me with people who always look out for me. You have given me family and friends who bless me every day with kind words and actions. They lift me up in ways that keep my eyes focused on you and make my spirit soar.*

Also, thank you, Lord, for keeping me safe. You protect me from those things that seem to haunt others. You help me make better choices, and you have provided me with advisors that help me with the difficult decisions. You speak to me in so many ways so that I always know you are here.

And Lord, I am so grateful for keeping those around me safe and loved. I hope that you provide me with the ability and sense to show them every day how much they matter. I hope that you give me the ability to give to them the same kindness they have provided to me. I am just so grateful for all of your blessings in my life, Lord. I pray that you remind me of just how lucky I am, and that you never allow me to forget to show my gratitude in prayer and returned kind acts. Thank you, Lord. In your name I pray, Amen.

Just as Melina had finished her prayer, Grant rushed into the waiting area. She rose from her chair and ran into Grant's arms sobbing tears of happiness. Grant held her tightly as he nuzzled her neck.

"Our baby girl is back… she came back to us," he whispered, his voice filled with emotion.

"Yes she is honey. We are so blessed because we have our Nikki back," Melina softly whispered back.

Danielle had shown up at the hospital to see if Nikki was still in a coma. She had heard when Dr. Khumalo was paged to come to her niece's room and followed him. The doctor went into the room and she stopped outside of the door and peered through the small window on the door. Danielle watched through the window until she finally could see that Nikki was actually awake. She gently eased the door open enough to listen to what was being said and heard the doctor when he said that Nikki seemed to not have any memory loss. Danielle quickly turned and headed out of the hospital. When she made it to her car and got inside, she slammed the door angrily.

"That little bitch… she woke up," Danielle thought to herself. *"She should have stayed in a coma. I know that she's*

going to tell her parents. I'm going to go home and pack up my shit and move into a hotel across town until I'm ready to finish carrying out my plans for my sister Melina."

Dr. Khumalo approached Melina and Grant and updated them on Nikki's condition.

"Nikki appears to be fine. She is very responsive, alert and appears to have no major memory loss. There are still a few more tests I want to do, but by all indications… she is well on her way to a full recovery. Nikki is asking for you both so go in and see her but don't tire her too much okay?" Dr. Khumalo said smiling.

When Melina and Grant rushed to Nikki's room and pushed open the door and she was lying there smiling her beautiful, captivating smile.

"Mama? Daddy?" Nikki said softly. "I'm so happy to see you both."

Melina and Grant approached their daughter's bedside, one on each side. They each took a hand and gently kissed it.

"You can't be any happier than we are right now baby," Melina said with tears rolling down her face.

"Baby girl… both your mother and I have missed you terribly and wasn't sure if we would get you back. We thank God that he did give you back," Grant said seating himself next to her on the bed.

"Mama… Daddy… I had been trying to fight my way back to you all for a long time. I love both of you,"

Nikki said looking from one to the other. "But I really need to tell you all something very important," Nikki said gathering her thoughts.

"What is it sweetie?" Melina said reassuringly, gently stroking Nikki's face.

"Yes what is baby girl?" Grant said attentively.

"This is going to be hard to believe… but Aunt Dannie tried to kill me. She shoved me down the stairs to stop me from exposing her," Nikki said, searching her parents' faces for a reaction.

Grant's face showed a bit of uncertainty and he became a bit nervous because he was hoping that Nikki hadn't meant she had found out about him and Danielle's indiscretions.

"What are you saying baby girl?" he asked in a non-believing tone.

"You think that your aunt tried to kill you?" Melina asked.

"Yes… Aunt Dannie did try to kill me. I had gotten suspicious of her after I had seen her go into you and daddy's bedroom one night that I knew you were at work," Nikki explained.

Grant gently laid Nikki's hand back on the bed and slowly eased away over to one corner of the room.

"Okay Nikki… you have my attention. Tell me more," Melina said, urging Nikki to continue.

After seeing Aunt Dannie go into you and daddy's bedroom that night, Xandria and I began paying more attention to her. Then we began following her around when she would act suspicious and saw her and daddy go into some hotels together a few times. I didn't say anything then because I wanted to be certain of what I was seeing mama. When I was convinced of what she was doing, I confronted her and told her that I was going to you. We argued at the top of the stairs near my room. I turned to leave and my aunt grabbed me by the arm. She told me that I would not tell anybody anything and then she shoved me down the stairs," Nikki sobbed.

"Oh-my-gosh sweetheart… I can't believe that my own sister would do something so heinous to my baby. I believe you sweetheart. I knew something has been off for some time but I didn't know what it was… I just couldn't put my finger on it. Never in my wildest imagination would I have thought that my sister could do something so vicious and cruel. I am so sorry that she did this to you," Melina said consoling her daughter. "Sweetheart… I love you very much and I will take care of this okay? I want you to do something very important for me… get you some rest and I will be back to see you tomorrow. I promise you… I will be back."

"Okay mama. I do feel a little tired. I love you too," Nikki said as she began drifting off into peaceful sleep.

Melina slowly walked over to Grant where he was still standing over in the corner of the room. He could barely look at her as the guilt inside consumed him.

"How could you do something like this Grant," Melina whispered angrily. "We are going home and finish this discussion. Wait for me in the car."

Grant walked over to his daughter and softly kissed her forehead and then turned and left the room. Melina got on her phone and called the police. She wanted to let them know that Nikki had just come out of her coma. Also, she wanted to tell the police that the accident at the house wasn't really an accident and that her sister Danielle had tried to kill her daughter.

Melina had spoken to officer Perelli. He had been the same officer who had booked Grant a few months back when he had been charged with strangulation.

"Where is Danielle now?" officer Perelli asked.

"Well she had been staying at my house. As far as I know, she could be there right now. I'm on my way home now but I did want to tell you about all of this. Also, you will have to talk to my daughter Nikki tomorrow to get a statement because she is resting now and I don't want her disturbed.

Melina joined Grant outside and they drove home. After arriving home, Melina angrily questioned Grant about Danielle.

"Grant... did you sleep with my sister? Was all of what Nikki said the truth? And don't lie to me."

Grant still couldn't bring himself to look at Melina. But he realized that he owed her the truth.

"Damn it Grant… look at me and tell me the truth. Have you and my sister been sleeping together behind my back?"

Grant turned to look at Melina with remorse written all over his face. He could see the anger and hurt in her eyes and couldn't believe that he had hurt and betrayed her this way.

"Yes Melina… I did sleep with Danielle but it wasn't like you think."

"Well how about you tell me how it was then."

"It was late and I had been sleep for a while. The lights were off and I was awakened by someone who I had presumed was you snuggling up to me in bed. I thought that maybe you had come home early and wanted to be with me. I never tried to see if it was you because who else would be getting into our bed. I turned over and began responding to who was touching and caressing me. I only found out that it wasn't you when I heard the voice of the person. By that time I had been making love to that person," Grant explained. "I found out then that it was Danielle."

"Why didn't you get up and throw her out of our room and out of our house?"

"Danielle decided that she would blackmail me into continuing to have sex with her by threatening to tell you. I didn't want you to ever know that I had done something so despicable and immoral because I was ashamed."

"Grant… if you had told me back then, we probably could have worked through it but you chose to hide it and go along with her sick, demented idea."

Grant dropped his head and sighed heavily to gather his thoughts before he continued. He knew that this would be the hardest thing he ever had to do but he had to tell Melina everything at this point.

"It gets worst Melina… much worst."

"How can anything be worst that you having an affair with my sister?"

Grant stared at Melina blankly and tried to force the words out but they seem to just get caught in his throat.

"Come on Grant… spit it out," Melina demanded.

"Danielle is pregnant with my child."

Melina stumbles backwards as if Grant's words seem to literally slap her in the face. She could barely stand, her heart felt as though it had been ripped from her chest, and her throat ached with unbearable pain. Melina couldn't believe the words that had come from Grant's mouth. This was the coup de gras that finally killed their marriage. Grant attempted to reach out to Melina but he was deflected by her rejection and cold, harsh words.

"Don't you dare touch me? You make my skin crawl," Melina said pulling away. "You are so despicable to me… so vial. What husband would do that to their wife? And you did it with my own sister? You are leaving this house tonight. I can't stand looking at you," Melina snarled.

Melina and Grant's argument was interrupted by a loud thump down the hallway. Immediately Melina knew that it was Danielle and rushed to her room.

"D-A-N-I-E-L-L-E! Open this damn door," Melina screamed banging on the door with her fist.

Suddenly the doorbell rang and Grant went to answer the door. It was officer Perelli.

"Why are you here officer Perelli," Grant asked.

"I came to pick up Danielle Jackson for questioning in regard to your daughter Nikki's fall."

Officer Perelli heard the loud banging and yelling down the hall and ran towards the sounds with Grant right on his heels. He found Melina yelling through the door.

"Melina… is Danielle in there?" he asked.

"I think so but she hasn't come to the door yet. I'm going to kill her," Melina shouted.

"Calm down Melina okay? I will handle it from here… I promise."

"Danielle… This is officer Perelli… I need you to come out right now. I have to take you down town for questioning."

"Okay… okay… I'm coming out, but you keep that bitch-ass sister of mine out of my way."

"Just come on out Danielle," the officer cited again.

"Alright… alright… I'm coming."

Danielle slowly opened the door and came out. Officer Perelli took her by the arm and began walking her out of the house. Melina lunged at her but Grant restrained her.

"You filthy bitch… I'm going to kill you. How could you put your hands on my child and then sleep with my husband?" Melina yelled, as the officer escorted Danielle from the house.

Melina jerked herself free from Grant, faced him and gave him the most worst look of contempt.

"Don't you ever grab me like that again? You pack you shit and get the hell out of my house," Melina yelled as she turned and stomped off upstairs to Nikki's room. "You had better not be still here when I get up in the morning."

That night Melina slept in her daughter's room because she felt closer to Nikki there. She had a larger than life chocolate, brown, teddy bear sitting in the middle of her bed. Melina crawled into her daughter's bed and wrapped her arms around the bear as the tears flowed without restriction. She drifted off into a peaceful slumber… escaping all of the horrible, hurtful events of this night.

Chapter

Twenty Four

The next morning Melina woke up in a haze. As she sat up on the side of the bed, the memories of last night began flooding her mind. Grant, the man who she had loved so much had committed the ultimate betrayal. But Grant had not been in this betrayal alone. Her sister Danielle was some piece of work and had to take responsibility for her role in this affair. Melina felt as though the whole thing was double betrayal because the affair was with a family member... a close family member. She is so distraught and the emotional intensity is compounded. Not only will she feel abandoned but she also feels replaced by someone better, younger, more attractive. Her pain is nearly unbearable because she feels that she has lost the position of importance in the life of her husband because of the betrayal and her feelings of failure as a wife.

Melina had to muster up the strength to visit Nikki and temporarily place her problems on the back burner. She had not seen Grant since their argument last night and assumed he had left the house as requested.

With her mind focusing on her daughter, Melina felt that Nikki needed her and she was not about to let her down especially since God had so graciously given her back to her. She was determined to make Danielle pay for all of the destruction she had caused in her life. A light bulb suddenly appeared over her head and the idea miraculously came to her. Somehow she would get Danielle to admit that she tried to kill her daughter. Melina went through the motions of showering and changing clothes and was on her way to the hospital.

Upon arriving at the hospital, Melina finds Nikki sitting up in bed and talking with officer Perelli.

"Nikki… I think that this will be all we need for now. You have signed off on all of the paperwork and charges will be filed against Danielle Jackson for attempted murder," Officer Perelli stated and then turned to leave the room.

"Officer Perelli!" Melina said with a slight bow of her head.

"How are you today Mrs. Harrington?" the officer said.

"I feel like I'm in a dream that I can't awake from right now," Melina replied.

"Well that's totally understandable," Officer Perelli said, pausing momentarily. "I'm going to head back to the station and get these reports filed on behalf of your daughter."

Melina takes two steps forward and then abruptly stops and turns to face the officer.

"Officer Perelli?"

Officer Perelli stops and turns to face Melina showing an attentive expression on his face.

"Yes Mrs. Harrington."

"Make sure that Danielle stays in jail where she cannot hurt my daughter again. I will be down there later because I need to speak with her."

"Of course Mrs. Harrington," the officer said with a slight nod, and then turns and leaves the room.

Melina walks up to Nikki and gives her a loving hug. She smiles warmly at her as she whisks a long, stray hair from her face.

"How are you feeling today sweetheart?" Melina asks.

"I feel better Mama," Nikki said repositioning herself on the bed. "You look kind of tired and stressed out mama. Are you okay?"

A distant look shrouded Melina's face as she thought of how to answer her daughter's question. Nikki and

Melina didn't keep secrets from each other and knew that her daughter sensed that something was amiss.

"What's wrong Mama?"

A soft sigh escaped Melina's lips as she prepared to reply.

"Your father and I had a huge blowup last night. I confronted him about being seen with Danielle at motels and he admitted to the affair with your aunt Dannie."

Melina's breathing quickened and a huge lump formed in her throat as she prepared herself to continue with her story.

"There's even worst news sweetie. Your father has gotten your aunt pregnant and she's been blackmailing him for months to continue the affair. At that point, I blew up… just couldn't deal with none of it. I asked him to leave the house and I'm not sure if we can get through this situation," Melina explains.

"Oh Mama… I'm so sorry. I didn't know about the baby but I did a little more time to get used to the idea that Daddy was having an affair. I love Daddy and always will but he was wrong for doing that to you. Daddy came by to see me this morning and I told him that he was wrong. Even though I love him it doesn't excuse what he did to you. Mama… whatever you decide to do I will support you okay?"

"I know that you will sweetheart," Melina said admirably eyeing her daughter.

Melina sits on the bed closely to her daughter's side and then pulls her hands into hers. A stray forms and then slides slowly down her cheek.

"You have grown up into such a beautiful, intelligent young woman. I am so proud to be your mom and so thankful that I am. You have made me proud of what you have become. You are the one that is first on my mind and the one that I pray for most of the time. Thank you for showing me respect… for honoring me with your character, and for loving the Lord Jesus as I had taught you. I am proud to be your mother everyday of the year and thankful for the love you give me and that I hold so dear. I love you more than life itself and I feel so blessed that God sent you to be my child… he could not have given me anyone else better. I know that you were divinely made in order for me to be so very blessed for seventeen wonderful years."

Melina paused for a moment, leaned in and kissed Nikki gently on the forehead. Then she continued.

"Your heart is filled with compassion, forgiveness, honesty and truth. It's all those traits that make you a good person… you always hold your head up and stand tall even when faced with the life's tough lessons. No matter how many times you were knocked down you would get right back up and move on. I also thank your friends… especially Xandria, that helped you through this! You're so blessed to have Xandria who has stood by you through thick and thin. You can always tell your true friends and family in times like these. So Nikki, you are moving in the right direction and I know you have the right tools to make it in whatever you do! Thank you for being you and always remember I love you and I am so very proud to be your mother!"

"Oh Mama… you are going to make me cry. I love you too just as much and there isn't anything that I wouldn't do for you."

Dr. Khumalo entered Nikki's room.

"Good morning! And how is my patient today?" the doctor asked.

"I feel so much better today so when can I go home?"

"Whoa-a-a-a! Let's slow down a little bit Nikki. We do want to keep you here a little longer to make sure that you continue improving. It shouldn't be long because you are doing so well. Try to bear with me a bit longer and let me perform more tests and monitor you okay? Today is Monday. If you are still doing well by the weekend, we can look at maybe letting you go home."

"Yes… yes… yes," Nikki said happily.

"I will check in on you a little later Nikki," Dr. Khumalo said with a wink as he exited the room.

"Sweetheart… I need to leave right now but I will be back in a few hours. I want to go to the police station and speak with officer Perelli okay? I also brought your cell phone and it's on the table next to your bed."

"Okay Mama," Nikki said retrieving her phone. "I'm going to call Xandria."

"Alright baby… I'll see you later," Melina said waving goodbye to her daughter.

Melina left the hospital and headed for the police station downtown. After arriving there, Melina asked to see Danielle but also wanted to discuss a plan to get her sister to confess to her crime. She told the officer that she wanted to wear a wire. Officer Perelli questioned her a bit because he wanted to be really sure that she wanted to do this deed.

Never waiving from her initial decision, Melina had a wire attached to her. The officer led her to a small interview room to wait while he went to get Danielle. The room had a small table and two chairs in it. Melina seated herself at the table with her back facing the door and waited anxiously for her sister to arrive. She felt her anger begin to bubble in her veins but she tried very hard to squelch it.

Within a few minutes the officer returned to the room with a handcuffed Danielle. He removed the cuffs and left the room closing the door behind him.

"Well, well, well… if it isn't my big sister Melina. What the hell are you doing here?" Danielle said sarcastically.

Melina was still seated at the table with her back to Danielle.

"I know about the affair Danielle… I know that you slept with Grant."

"Oh yeah? So! This time wasn't the first time that I screwed your husband. FYI… I slept with Grant when he was your fiancé too… back at our daddy's funeral," Danielle snapped.

Danielle walked around the table so that she could face Melina. Pulling out a chair, she plopped down in it, leaned back and began rubbing her stomach.

Melina was starting to lose control of her anger and was grinding on her teeth.

"You know what sis? I told you that this baby was my boyfriend's baby but it's not… it's Grant's. And that little nappy head ass daughter of yours was stupid for trying to threaten me. She said that she was going to tell you about what I had been doing and I wasn't going to allow that to happen. That's why I shoved her little ass down the stairs. Too bad she lived uh?"

Melina anger erupted. She shoved the chair backwards so hard that it flipped over, she stood straight up stared down upon Danielle.

"So you freely admit to hurting my child," Melina said trying to stifle the anger in her voice.

"Damn right I did it you stupid bitch… I pushed her ass down the stairs," Danielle gloated.

"Did you get that Perelli?" Melina yelled.

"I sure did," the officer replied.

"And now Danielle… I'm going to get you," Melina threatened.

Danielle saw an expression in Melina's eyes she had never seen before and it frightened her. She stood to try to leave but Melina had grabbed her by the arm, spun her around, and slapped her so hard that the sound echoed in the small room. Then she grabbed her little sister by the neck and shoved her backwards up against the wall. Melina slapped Danielle's face again even harder this time.

Melina trembled with anger toward her little sister but had to remind herself that she was pregnant. She raised her hand and pointed her trembling finger directly into Danielle's face… her finger so close that it was nearly touching her nose.

"If you ever think about touching my daughter again I will forget that you are my sister… all bets will be off, and I will treat you just as any other person in the streets. I will give you the worst ass whopping of your life. So you never ever come near me or my daughter for as long as you live. From this day forward I no longer have a sister. You go to H-E-L-L Danielle! YOU GO TO STRAIGHT TO HELL-L-L-L!" Melina screamed.

After hearing all of the commotion, Officer Perelli burst through the door and pulled Melina off of Danielle, placed the cuffs back on her and led her out of the room.

"I hate you Lina… I hate you. I will hate you forever," Danielle screamed as she was escorted from the room.

Chapter

Twenty Five

A Month Later

Dr. Khumalo had given Nikki a clean bill of health and allowed her to go home with the stipulation of taking it easy over the next week or two. Before long, the week or two had turned into a month. Melina's was so happy to have her daughter home and Nikki was glad to be home. She had blossomed into such a responsible, intellectual, young woman and was preparing to enter college. Their relationship simply had picked up where it left off. There was no relationship quite as primal as the one between a mother and her daughter and both loved each other so much. But the same can't be said for Melina's relationship with her husband Grant.

Grant had called Melina to make sure it was okay to stop by to visit with their daughter Nikki. After Nikki and her dad had their quality time together, Xandria had come by to see her best friend too. Grant was about to leave when Melina asked him to come into the kitchen so that they could discuss things between the two of them.

Ending their marriage was not easy, but it was for the best and it was necessary for Melina. It had not been a snap decision on her part, but she had put much thought and consideration into the decision over the past month. This contemplation stage she had gone through had given her the time to mentally work through the various emotions of dealing with her marriage to Grant and his infidelity with her sister Danielle.

The toughest thing about Melina's and Grant's relationship had been knowing when and how to end it. Both had committed to it believing it would never end. But for Melina realizing that it must end required a complete reversal of a genuine, well rooted, belief. She had trusted Grant's feelings for her and his commitment to their marriage. She used to have faith in their relationship, faith in her partner, and faith in their ability as a couple to withstand anything life threw at them. Melina and Grant had solidified their relationship with a child and property. Reality's erosive tremors, big and small, destabilized her faith gradually over the past months. When Melina finally admitted that not much of what she believed about her feelings for Grant and their relationship was true, what could she do? She knew that she would not be able to live in the ruins of a deceptive relationship. Some people choose to die in bad relationships but this could not be her.

"Grant… you know that we have to take responsibility for our mistakes, and forgive others for theirs, but know that that doesn't mean we have to live with them. We consider our options and what we're willing to sacrifice to gain freedom. I can't do this anymore," Melina said softly.

"Melina… I can't be angry with you because I did this to us. I should have been man enough to stand my ground and should have protected our relationship. I allowed Danielle to come between us. And for that I am so sorry," Grant confessed.

"I love you Grant but just can't live with you anymore so I'd like a divorce. I want us to work out the details unselfishly and with determination and patience so that everyone affected by it will be hurt as little as possible. I made this decision carefully considering all the consequences. I really believe that we can both resolve this and avoid adding mistakes to mistakes, and forming new intimate relationships until our emotions have stabilized and our families have adjusted to the change," Melina said sadly.

"I love you too Melina and probably always will but I can understand why you want to end our marriage. I really don't deserve you. So with that being said, I will not give you any resistance and will comply with your wishes," Grant promised.

Melina and Grant quietly got their divorce and both pursued their lives as single parents. Nikki and Melina stay in close touch even though Nikki is in college. Seasoned moms like Melina know for a fact that the typical day-to-day schedule leaves little time for heart-to-hearts but they do make the most of their times together.

There are tons of creative and fun ways for Melina and Nikki to stay connected even when they sometimes feel a little disconnected from each other. They plan a girls-only spa day complete with facials, makeup application and the requisite mani-pedi combo. At the end of their spa day, they both will be feeling relaxed, refreshed and updated on each other's lives. And they cap it off by ordering out for dinner. After all, they didn't want to ruin their sparkling new manicures, do they?

There were times that a vacay with Mom was the perfect opportunity to take all those trips that men in your family wouldn't be caught dead on. Melina and Nikki would keep it close to home by exploring the cultural offerings of Lincoln, like the ballet, theater or even the opera. Sometimes, they would splurge on a trip to one of the cultural and shopping Mecca's of the world, like New York City.

Melina got to enjoy the privilege of showing her daughter the phenomenon that is Bloomingdale's, haggle for deals on merchandise in Chinatown or hit as many Broadway shows as possible. Both women were bowled over by big-city offerings, making their trips both memorable and enjoyable.

If Melina and Nikki were not feeling the big city, they took road trips to the beach or just picked a nearby destination at random. All of that travel time gave them both ample opportunities to create plenty of new memories. Sometimes they would just stay home and enjoyed cooking up chef-worthy meals. Melina would share special family recipe meals such as her famous lasagna and apple crisp and she would let her daughter in on the family secrets. Plus, being elbow-deep in cookie dough was the perfect time for Melina to share stories about her own mother's cooking.

* * * * *

One of the many challenges that make divorce so complicated is that even while you're dealing with all the crud of the divorce process itself, you think about how you will get on with a new life for yourself and your children after divorce. Melina had made huge strides in this area with the support of her daughter Nikki, the church, and her strong belief in God.

Nikki had been in college for a year and was doing extremely well and she visited her mother Melina often. Grant supported Nikki also with whatever she needed in school and was just as generous with Melina. During the divorce and since both Melina and Grant remained very civil to each other but they each maintain their separate lives. She and Grant eventually got their relationship to a point to where they became great friends and both help with their daughter Nikki's needs.

Danielle had tried to cause problems for Grant after she was sent to prison for attempted murder but due to the justifying circumstances the charges were dismissed. After the baby was born, it was placed with a couple who desperately wanted a child. Melina was happy that the child had a chance for a good life because she knew that her little sister would never be able to put some else's needs above her own selfish ones.

Chapter

Twenty Six

Melina embraced her life without having a man around. Oftentimes, Melina came across songs that told a story and there was something about it that caused it to stay longer in her mind than other songs. She thought the reason for this was the story in and of itself made the song a whole lot more interesting and memorable. Occasionally she did think of the good times she had shared with Grant.

Some songs told stories about historical incidents that really happened. Others, especially blues songs, told more personal stories, about loved ones, fights, death but they all speak of people and the song contains a tale within it that has a beginning and an end. There has been one such song which came to mind for Melina and she often reflected on it and its meaning. Bobby "Blue" Bland wrote this song and as sad as it was it helped her as she continued the journey of living her life. Melina remembered these lyrics to Mr. Bland's moving and inspirational song. The song's title is *"You've Got to Hurt before You Heal"*.

When you lose the one you love your heart goes through changes, especially when your sweet memories still hold their thrill. And just when you think the pain is all gone don't fool yourself because here's the deal, that's the way love works you've got to hurt before you heal. You're going cry oh yes you're going to cry, and when the tears they may stop falling; they may stop falling all down your face but they still fall down your heart. You never know how long the wound it'll take to heal, it might take months but it could take years. But that's the way love works you've got to hurt before you heal.

The emotional pain inflicted on us by others can be far worse than the physical wounds we experience. So what is the right ointment for wounded hearts? Melina has this huge gaping hole in her heart that was left by Grant and her younger sister Danielle. She sometimes felt that this hole could never be filled Kand that she would be left with the hollow in her heart forever. The betrayal left by two people she loved most left her a broken woman. Even though she had this hole in her heart, she had to believe that there was still hope for her and that there was a Healer who would mend her broken heart. As David said in Psalms 147:3 - "He heals the brokenhearted and binds up their wounds." God wants to heal us of all of our wounds and we just have to allow him.

If you have ever had an injury or a deep cut, you know how painful it is and how it hurts to be touched. Oftentimes sorrow and loss are like deep wounds. They can be so painful that it seems no one or nothing can make the pain go away. Sometimes our heart is so broken that we can't even express the words and nothing seems to take the pain away.

People who try to encourage us can't seem to say the right thing. Like a deep wound, a broken heart will not heal overnight. Like some medicines that burn when you apply them to a skin wound, so can a well-meaning friend who says the wrong thing at the wrong time. Who wants to pour rubbing alcohol on an open wound? We search the stores to find an ointment that we can apply to our skin wound that will not burn and then cover it gently with a Band-Aid. It's the same way with our broken heart. We need the right ointment to bring about healing.

So what is the right ointment for our hearts? How do we begin to heal? How can the hole in our hearts that is gaping open begin to close?

Melina learned to recognize the pain and understand it is OK to hurt. Sometimes we seek to cover the pain by ignoring it or through other means like the use of alcohol or drugs, which will only cause us to get infected and reverse the healing process. Like a deep skin wound, we must apply the right ointment or a Band-Aid so we can begin to heal or else it can get infected and become worse. We cannot ignore our pain and think it will go away. Understand that it is OK to hurt. We try to push the hurt away, but we can't. The hurt isn't outside of us—it's inside. So, in our attempt to push the hurt away, we actually push the hurt deeper inside. We then can spend the rest of our life running from this suppressed hurt. By going through our hurts, we are a part of the human race—millions of people who are going through similar pains. It is during this time that we need a lot of love, encouragement and hope restored. We realize how frail we are and see our great need for God. It is a time to reflect on the true meaning of life and the greatest opportunity of all to draw close to God. It is an opportunity to learn empathy toward others who are going through the same things. You cannot do all of these things if you try to ignore the pain.

Melina had decided to seek out the Healer. Seek God as your healer! Just like you tell a doctor your symptoms, tell God how much you were wounded and need His healing touch. He will hear the cries of the broken. God the Father wants to reach down, take your hand, and walk you through your pain. It may take weeks. For many of us it will take years, perhaps even a lifetime to close the wounds of our hearts completely. God will spend as much time and as many years as necessary to help you through it. He wants to gently apply the daily salve or ointment of His Holy Spirit to your heart until your heart is healed.

Melina reached out to others during her time of healing. As God has reached out to us, so we should be an instrument of God to reach out and help others who are in pain. Ask God to use you to encourage others through their pain. By your own pain you will be able to understand and help in a far greater way. Christ our Savior was in all points tested and understands all that you go through. He reached out to us by giving His life so that we would be healed. By reaching out to others, our own pain will begin to disappear; the holes in our hearts will begin to close. Healing takes time.

After a few years, there is still a hole in Melina's heart, but it's much smaller because of God. Every time she felt God's presence, every time she saw God's intervention in her life, every time she reached out to help someone in need, she imagined that hopefully one day she would be blessed to have someone else enter into her life again. Sometimes it is the ones that you hold nearest and dearest to your heart are the ones who hurt you the most. But you still need to continue to live, laugh, love, and enjoy life.